TAMING HER COWBOY BILLIONAIRE

BROTHERS OF MILLER RANCH BOOK FIVE

NATALIE DEAN

KENZO PUBLISHING

DEDICATION

I'd like to dedicate this book to YOU! The readers of my books. Without your interest in reading these heartwarming stories of love, I wouldn't have made it this far. So thank you so much for taking the time to read any and hopefully all of my books.

And I can't leave out my wonderful mother, son, sister, and Auntie. I love you all, and thank you for helping me make this happen.

Most of all, I thank God for blessing me on this endeavor.

EXCLUSIVE BOOKS BY NATALIE DEAN

CONTENTS

1

Bryant

For a wedding celebration, the reception was pretty lame.

Or at least, in Bryant's opinion it was, but no one asked his opinion. In fact, no one was even really talking to him, leaving him sitting at the friends-and-family table that was more "friends" and less "family."

It was whatever, though. Bryant was used to it as the youngest and the one who chose not to follow the oh-so-holy—*boring*—path that all of his siblings had. Whenever he saw his parents, there were sad smiles and questions about if he was coming home. His brothers had no problems telling him how much he was hurting folks with his wild lifestyle. Well, except Bradley.

The two of them had always shared more of a bond than with the others. As the youngest pair and "different" than their brothers, he'd always assumed they'd be a pair forever. But when Bradley chose to stay on the Ranch while going to college online, specializing in finance, that had pretty much ended that.

Still, when Bradley asked Bryant to show up for Benji's wedding—not be in the party, just show up—he found himself saying yes. Even though he knew the event would be some lame, stuck-up, and altogether boring affair.

There wasn't even *alcohol*. Who had a wedding without alcohol? If it weren't for the flask in his suit jacket, he wouldn't know what to do with himself.

But the flask would be getting low eventually, so he needed some new entertainment and fast.

Finding something to hold his attention shouldn't have been so hard, after all, the whole Miller clan was there along with whatever hick family the bride had. But it seemed that everyone either knew of him or had heard of him and were giving him a wide berth. Like he was some incubus come to seduce them from their pious ways.

Please. Like any of them were up to his standards.

Well, that wasn't *quite* true. All of his brothers had managed to snatch some really fine women. Even Benji's girl was beautiful, although Bryant would never admit to that in public. After all, in his world it was fine to like bigger women behind closed doors, but outside was meant for models and more acceptable folks.

His world being reality, not the little Christian fantasy land his family had carved out for themselves.

Ugh, he needed some more punch.

Getting up, he walked over to the table with the stupid nonalcoholic punch and poured himself a glass before tilting in some of the contents of his flask. There had to be at least one hot chick to distract himself with who wasn't all cozied up to his brothers.

It really was something. After all of the Miller boys being single for most of their adult lives—except for that one girl Bradley dated for a while who turned out to be a gold digger—suddenly all of his brothers were snatched up. The matching up had started four years ago, when Bryant was twenty-four and had just graduated from his Master's program—that he paid for himself.

Ben was first, with his high school sweetheart who he never got over. That chick was hot, especially for being as old as his eldest brother, and was making a name for herself online. She was also so pregnant, he was surprised that she didn't pop right out of her bridesmaid's dress.

Then Bart, his next brother, ended up with a girl who had a body like a Coke bottle and was the daughter of the town drunk. Bryant had thought maybe his brothers had relaxed their standards. But *nope*, turned out she fit in with them like a glove, all church-going and pure and blah, blah, blah. Kind of a waste to have a body like *that* on a goody-two-shoes who didn't know how to use it, but he supposed some people were just determined to waste their potential.

Then there was the real big girl that was in the wedding gown staring at Benji like he was the sun. Bryant had always suspected his brother had a thing for larger women, so he wasn't surprised that he ended up with a lady who was muscular and could intimidate any man. And Bryant meant that in a completely hot way.

And lastly there was Bradley. Weird, not very social, super into theater and reading, good with numbers but not emotions. For a long while Bryant didn't think Bradley would find anyone. Not because he was *so* weird that no one found him desirable, but because he seemed completely uninterested in any romance at all. There had been whispers that maybe the penultimate son was gay, but Bryant could tell that wasn't the reason. Humans either bored his brother or irritated him.

And yet even he was engaged, to this tiny little thing who always wore clothes three times her size and jumped at the slightest of sounds like she was worried she had a bomb strapped to her.

Five brothers, and four taken. What a strange world. And Bryant definitely wasn't going to be changing that ratio anytime soon. He was just twenty-eight, after all. He had his choice of so many hotties and beautiful women, why would he ever tie himself down to just one? It'd be a waste!

And everyone knew that a true sin was wastefulness, so really, he was the holiest of the Millers in a certain light.

Even he had to snort at that. He was many things, but holy wasn't one of them. He was rich, charming—if he said so himself—handsome and did he mention rich? Usually women would be salivating all over him whenever he attended an event. But here? Nope. It was beginning to grate on his nerves that there wasn't a single person around who wasn't hooked on that whole Jesus fandom.

His eyes swept over the room once more, taking in the older, somewhat familiar faces, the disapproving looks and that particular sort of posture that seemed to come specifically from living in the same small town one's whole life.

It wasn't until he reached the dance floor that he finally saw something, the briefest flicker of light among so many fuddy-duddies.

She was dancing with one of his cousins, a young boy of five or six who knew exactly how adorable he was. The woman was bordering on tall with her heels, and cut a slender, feminine figure in her bridesmaid's dress.

He hadn't noticed her during the ceremony, but maybe that was because he hadn't been paying much attention. He'd been texting one of his hookups, trying to arrange for something once he jetted from his familiar obligation, so sue him.

Interest rising, Bryant crossed over to them, dodging hicks and rednecks alike who definitely had no idea that his suit cost twelve thousand dollars. He knew he probably shouldn't have worn one of his designer suits at an event where no one had the class or tact to be appreciative, but he had a brand, and that brand was being covered in name brands. He couldn't bring himself to wear something off-the-rack.

Finally, he reached the two without any moonshine being dumped on him and bent down, offering a dollar to the little guy.

"Hey, why don't you let me cut in?"

The kid looked at the dollar like it might as well have been a cool hundred, and snatched it, jetting off with practically a lane of fire after him. But when Bryant straightened to turn his charm onto the woman, she just fixed him with a polite smile.

"Thank you for the break. My feet were really starting to ache, but that boy is just too adorable to refuse."

She was even prettier up close, but in a way that he wasn't used to.

Now that he was closer, he could see that she was at least partially some sort of Asian, with her almond-shaped eyes and heart-shaped face. She was pale, incredibly so, and her long hair was done up on top of her head in a neat bun surrounded by complicated looking braids. She wore makeup, but only a slight amount. Just enough to let you know that she had indeed dressed up for the occasion but wasn't much interested in wearing a full face.

Before Bryant could put together a proper name for whatever look she was giving off, she turned on her low heel and crossed to one of the closest empty tables.

Well, that was strange.

While he knew that some of these people weren't exactly fond of him, that they prayed over his lost soul, he wasn't used to people having such a blasé reaction to meeting him face-to-face. Usually they either compensated for their mean thoughts by being overly nice, or they outright demanded that he apologize to his parents and return to the fold.

Without his mind processing it, he followed her, sitting in the seat next to her at the table. She didn't seem to pay him any mind, using one of the napkins to blot at the back of her slender neck.

There was a strange sort of... fragility to her. She was thin, bordering on waifish, like a nymph or dryad that wasn't supposed to be seen by men. Was she some sort of fainting rose? A delicate little princess who never had to work outside? Not his usual type, but she was stunningly beautiful and at the moment, that was enough.

"Hi, I'm Bryant," he said, sliding his hand across the table to her.

The woman looked at his offered limb, set her napkin down, and gave him that same sweet, polite smile.

"I am well aware of who you are, Bryant Miller."

Ah, so she was playing coy, was she? Now that was something he knew how to deal with. He leaned in slightly, just enough for there to be an air of intimacy but not enough that he was invading her personal space. But as he moved closer, he caught the faintest scent of something lovely. Melon and some sort of flower maybe, sweet and soft and refreshing. Was that her? His mind went to unholy places. Maybe, if he played his cards right...

"Oh, does my reputation proceed me?"

"I highly doubt you'd go anywhere if your reputation wasn't already there, making introductions for you."

"And you know so much about my life?" Who was this woman? Bryant realized that she was definitely no wilting flower.

She stared at him, calm and pleasant, but there was an underlying steel to her. Bryant thought it would do him well not to underestimate her.

And that thought sent a strange sort of thrill through him.

...that was also weird.

"Well, I do have access to a computer with a search engine, despite what you may think of us small-town folk."

"Glad to know that Blackfish County has made it into the twenty-first century."

"Yes, considering the difficulty that many rural areas have with getting stable internet, we certainly are blessed."

"Ah, so political, are we?" Bradley asked as he leaned in a little more. "Or do you just have a special place in your heart for Wi-Fi?"

"Isn't there a phrase for this?" the woman replied, the tiniest, *tiniest* of smirks curling the corner of her pinkish lips. "Never discuss politics, sex, or religion at a wedding?"

"Well, I've never been much for rules."

"So I've heard."

Bryant chuckled, resting on his elbow. "You seem to know so much about me, and yet I know so little of you."

"Because you ask so little of me."

"Fair enough. What's your name, beautiful?"

"Keiko," she answered before affixing him with a steadier look. "And may I ask you a question?"

"It's only fair since I've been asking you all of them."

"What is it about your family that makes you want to get back at them so much?"

"Pardon?" Bryant asked, blinking at her. He expected some inquiry to any one of his borderline legendary exploits. Or a whispered request of if what they said was true about him. But she skipped right over that and headed straight towards something he hadn't anticipated at all.

"It would be one thing if you were just living the way you want to and they happened to disagree—although I know that's a part of it—but you *like* coming here, and you *like* doing things you specifically know will bother them. You enjoy telling your brothers about your escapades or making sure they somehow find out.

"That doesn't just come out of nowhere. You're paying them back for something. A misdeed, or maybe even a series of misdeeds. So what I'd like to know is, what exactly set you off, all those years ago?"

Bryant stared at her, blinking slightly. No one had ever asked him anything remotely along those lines. He wasn't sure anyone would even know to, but she was just sitting there, looking at him with that same polite disinterest.

"Ah, I see that I might have overstepped. In any case, it was nice meeting you, Bryant." She dipped her head then headed back to the wedding party table, leaving Bryant to watch her as she exited.

...who *was* that woman?

2

Keiko

She could feel his eyes on her for the rest of the reception.

Keiko certainly hadn't meant to come face-to-face with the youngest Miller son, the one she had heard so many stories about that she had almost wondered if he was real or some sort of legend like Big Foot. She'd seen him maybe in passing at a family get-together or two, but nothing substantial.

To be completely honest, she found the whole idea of the Miller prodigal son fascinating. As far as she could tell, the Millers were some of the most honest, accepting, and loving people she'd ever met. And even though their disappointment in Bryant was clear, none of them seemed to hate him. She always wondered what it would be like to pick the brain of someone who was so determined to defy everything good that he was surrounded by.

But what she'd never expected was for him to walk right up to her and ask her for a dance.

She supposed stranger things had happened, but she was hard-pressed to think of any as he looked at her with those patently intense Miller eyes and smooth grin. He was different than his brothers. Less rugged, more polished and classy, but there was also a sort of... a hunger to him.

His essence crawled up her spine and licked out over her brain. A couple of words from him was all it took for her to confirm that she was looking at a man who didn't know what it felt like to be satisfied. To be happy. He was a life-junkie, always chasing the next thrill, the next challenge, the next chunk of pleasure to numb himself until that hunger came rolling back in.

The life-junkie hunger wasn't exactly a foreign feeling to her. She knew how that endless cycle could be, caught in a wheel that was constantly spinning, dying to find something that would give a moment's relief. But she knew where her issues stemmed from; the question was, what had started Bryant on that path?

But then she'd realized that perhaps her best friend's wedding was not the appropriate venue to dissect whatever made the man in front of her tick, so she'd dismissed herself as politely as she could.

And yet his eyes stayed on her.

She was used to blatant staring. She and her mother were the only Asians in their entire town and one of a handful of people of color. Keiko was also aware that she was aesthetically pleasing enough to warrant a few turned heads, and then add on top of it her role in the church... Well, that definitely had allowed her to grow acclimated with people letting their gaze linger for too long.

But this Bryant fellow's attention was different. His stare was intense—as most of the Millers were when they were focused. His gaze was like a tangible pressure across her entire body that made the hair on the back of her neck stand up. But it wasn't aggressive. Otherwise, she would go over to him and say something. No. It was just... curious, in a way. But also relentless.

"Thanks for holding the baby in until after the ceremony."

Keiko shook her head, bringing herself back to the real world to see Dani was leaning towards Chastity, who was leaning back in her chair and rubbing her very distended stomach.

"Oh, I don't know," the darker-skinned woman said. "I still have an hour or two to crank this little guy out."

"Oh please," Missy said with that drawl she only used when she was particularly relaxed and happy. "Like you would ever ruin this outfit by breaking your water all over it."

Chastity turned ashen, which wasn't like her, and pushed her plate away. "All right. New rule. No talking of any bodily fluids around the very pregnant lady." She groaned and let her head tilt back, her dark, dark hair tumbling down to almost touch the floor. "And also remind me to never get pregnant again."

Keiko couldn't help but grin at that. While it had certainly been an interesting experience being with Chastity through her entire pregnancy, it had definitely enforced her decision to never, ever have children biologically. Sometimes, when she was especially tired or stressed, it felt like she barely had control over her own body. She couldn't imagine if some little mini-human lived inside of her, making her do things she didn't want to or had no control over, like spontaneously losing her breakfast or gaining so much weight.

Keiko blanched at that and looked down at her own,

unused plate. She had been so busy dancing and having fun that she hadn't tried any of the catering yet. And she really should. The best way to stay healthy was to have a routine, and her routine involved four to five small meals a day.

"Well, I don't know about y'all, but I could still use some grub." Missy looked to Keiko. "Wanna come up with me?"

Keiko felt a warmth flow through her. Missy knew exactly what she was doing, and Keiko appreciated her for that.

One of the most difficult things about being in recovery from an eating disorder was the utter lack of motivation to feed herself. Especially since food's textures and smells could be... *off-putting*. But if her friend was asking her to accompany *them* to get food, suddenly the whole thing grew easier. Dani called it the care-giver override, and Keiko had to agree with the sentiment.

"Oh, while you're at it, will you get me a rib and some okra?" Dani handed over her plate.

Keiko took it gratefully. She always did best with a task to complete. Kept her mind in order and her anxiety at bay.

"Of course."

She and Missy walked over to the table, grabbing what they wanted. Despite the tall girl loading up her plate with a truly shocking amount of food, she didn't make a single comment on what Keiko chose to eat, and that was a relief in and of itself. For someone who never struggled with an eating disorder, Missy certainly seemed understanding.

Then again, maybe it was all her experience with Bart. Not that PTSD and anorexia were all that related, but still, both were mental disorders that made people hurt themselves. Or maybe Missy was just really good with taking care of everyone. Either way, Keiko was grateful.

Her entire life, her only friend had really been Dani.

Someone whom Keiko had fiercely admired ever since they were young. When they had first met, Keiko had thought the robust girl was everything that she herself wasn't, and she so desperately wanted to be more like her. She liked to think that she had done a pretty good job so far, but she had such a long way to go.

It didn't help that most people seemed to think of her as some sort of permanently gracious pillar of calm. If anything, she was constantly brimming with energy and anxiety that she was always trying to reason out and suppress.

And that was *exhausting.*

The pressure to appear perfectly fine was one of the reasons she volunteered so much at the church. Helping others and giving acts of service was one of the few things that gave her peace outside of her small circle of friends. She found it was easier to feel the presence of God there, to rely on his hand and guidance.

If only that feeling could last beyond the church doors.

She supposed it might help if she was more open about her struggles, but she so often found people judgmental and closed off. After all, how much had Dani been bullied even into her adult years? And from what Keiko had heard, Missy had fared even worse. Even Chastity, the sweet and beautiful girl that everyone seemed to admire, got all sorts of hateful comments online. The haters would tell her to go back to her country or be surprised that she spoke English so well. The irony of telling a Native American woman all that was lost to the anonymous faces of the web.

No. She was just fine with only her girlfriends, her parents, and her therapist knowing.

She rejoined the table with Missy right beside her, sliding Dani a plate with exactly what she asked for. The bride flashed her a grin, but only got to take about a bite or so before her new hubby insisted she get up and dance with him for what was apparently "their song."

The gesture was beautifully sweet and saccharine in that perfect way that Keiko had always thought was silly. Then again, romance had never been much of her thing. Between her journey with mental illness, education, and her time with the church, she didn't have time for much else.

"Isn't it sweet?" Missy said around the entire chicken wing she had in her mouth.

Keiko had seen the trick plenty of times before, but it was still something else to watch the blond draw it out of her mouth with all of the meat gone.

"Now we just have to get you a nice boy, Keiko."

Her stomach twisted at that, objecting to the wrongness. "I've never felt that I needed a relationship to be whole. Besides, I have far too much to do as it is."

Surprisingly, it was Sophia who raised her eyebrows and leaned in. It seemed with every month the newest woman to join the Miller household was becoming more and more of the person she was created to be.

"Like what?" Sophia said. "Afraid the parishioners are going to perish if you're not there to shepherd them to the coffee and bagels?"

She knew the young woman was just teasing, but it did hit a touch of insecurity in her. "I don't know, to be perfectly honest. I just feel like God has something in store for me. A test maybe, or a challenge. Or... something."

"That's not very specific."

"It's not supposed to be," she answered with a wan smile. While some people might interpret Sophia's forthrightness as rude, Keiko knew that she had spent so much of her life just barely surviving that she had to learn all sorts of things that most people took for granted. Especially when it came to faith, social cues, or finances.

Keiko continued, "That's part of it. The journey can be half of the challenge, and that's the beauty. But I'm determined to be ready for the challenges God sends my way once I do find them."

"Huh." Sophia sat back in her seat, fidgeting in her dress. "I'm not sure what to think of those excuses."

"That's all right." Keiko took a bite of the mashed potatoes and tried not to wince as her tongue hit a chunk of unwhipped spud. Textures set her off so easily. "I know exactly what *I* think about them. And I'm perfectly okay with it."

3

Bryant

*B*ryant was bored, *so* bored, so he did the only thing that made sense to him.

He drank.

His family would be angry if they knew about his secret flask of alcohol. But that didn't stop him. Their opinion of him never did. After being cut off by his family at the ripe ol' age of nineteen, Bryant Miller had built up a fortune of his own, and in the next few years or so his brand's worth was set to exceed his family's. Of course, they were too traditional and set in their ways to appreciate his particular brand of genius.

But when he wasn't drinking, or eating, he was watching the woman who had said all *that* to him. She was wrong, of course. She knew nothing about him. She was some Bible-thumper who got all of her money handed to her by someone else and probably only knew about him from tabloids. She wasn't anyone important. She'd never been in a magazine or featured online as an up-and-coming billionaire.

And yet... he was still staring.

She had to know he was. He made no attempt to hide it, because why should he? But she completely ignored him.

He wasn't used to being ignored.

So he drank more, trying to occupy his time until he could leave. The reception seemed to be taking *forever*, but it was probably because the backwater people of their small town had so little to look forward to that they had to draw out every party like it was their last.

"Hey, Bryant. Can we talk?"

Ugh. He knew that voice. How could he not know Ben, his older brother? The head of the new generation. The inheritor. He always took everything so *seriously*. He was such a buzzkill; it drove Bryant crazy. And even worse, he was predictable, which made him boring. He knew exactly what his eldest brother was going to say before the man's hand rested on his shoulder in that patronizing way of his.

"I haffa feelin' this isn't something I can say no to, huh?"

"Aw, come on now Bryant, are you drunk?"

"Aw, get off it, Ben. I'm just buzzed, and you're ruining it, in case ya were worried 'bout that."

"Come on, let's take a walk, shall we?"

Bryant hated how his older brother would just boss him around, and yet he found himself following. He didn't remember always resenting his brother. Once, he'd looked up to him. But somewhere around freshman year of high school that began to change. When Bryant could never measure up and all of the things that he liked just weren't what Millers were supposed to do.

"Whadda'ya want?" Bryant asked once they were in a far corner away from everything else.

Some small part of him, some stupid, logic-less part, hoped that his older brother would open his arms and say he was sorry. But of course, that wasn't what happened. Instead, Ben looked down at him with that holier-than-thou expression. Bryant felt his temper buck up.

"Look, I understand that it might have been fun and exciting to tomcat around, but you're nearly twenty-nine now. Don't you think it's time to come home and make things right? You know how much it hurts Ma and Pa to see you ruining yourself day in and day out."

Ugh. There it was again. The condescension. The certainty that they were right. It burned into Bryant like rejection, and he felt poison slide down his tongue and coat his words as they left his mouth.

"Come back home? Why would I do that when I'm twice as successful as all of you good little boys who stayed tied to Ma's apron strings *combined?* You settled, Ben. That doesn't mean I have to, and it doesn't mean you have the right to judge me."

"Bryant, I'm not judging—"

He held up a finger, growing too close to his brother's face as he spoke. "Now, now, big brother, it's not very Christian to *lie.*"

That seemed to strike something in him, and he looked from Bryant to the reception behind him. Sighing, his shoulders slumped, and he stepped to the side. "You know, one day I hope you get your head on straight. But in the meantime, not everyone is trying to attack you."

"Easy to say when you're the one who everyone loves."

If Ben had anything to say to that, Bryant didn't hear it,

already stumbling to the bathroom. Suddenly he was dizzy. So dizzy, and he couldn't recall where he saw the lavatory.

He tried to look for direction signs or a path, but everything was starting to get blurry and confusing. Well, it certainly looked like his light buzz was going a little further than he intended and he was careening straight towards drunk.

And not even happy drunk, which would have been fun. But that sour, pissy sort of drunk that made him feel... *Empty.*

Somehow, Bryant ended up outside, but that was okay with him because the air was cool on his face. Tilting his head upward, he looked at the twilight sky, watching as tones of royal blue and lilac bled into the warm, buttery orange and syrupy scarlet of the sunset.

If there was one thing he did miss about home, it was the sky. So open and beautiful and fresh, it was a reminder of how small he was in the grand scheme of everything. Of how he was just a tiny piece of a puzzle trying to scheme to make himself grander and larger than he needed to be. And somehow, that was comforting, even though it probably shouldn't have been.

The night sky was beautiful, and simple, in a perfect sort of way. Feeling at peace, Bryant stood there and watched until the sun fully sank into the sky, leaving stars to slowly pop into his vision, dotting the thick, obsidian blanket above him.

He spent quite a while standing there, but at least he could probably excuse himself and go to his hotel. Except he couldn't really remember what hotel he was even at. Or how he had even gotten to... where was he again?

Oh right. His brother's wedding.

Somehow, he was the only single Miller boy.

They were all a bunch of suckers.

Suckers? No, his mouth was too dry for candy. He needed a drink.

Turning, Bryant furrowed his brows and tried to guess where he came from. He remembered walking, then he was suddenly outside. But that certainly didn't make sense. He was so confused that he ended up just sort of roaming around until he heard a strange noise from somewhere.

No, not strange noise. Pretty noise. He liked it. He liked pretty things.

Smiling, he stumbled after it, realizing it was someone humming an unfamiliar tune. He wasn't sure what he was expecting, maybe a fairy, or a siren, or a high-quality Bluetooth speaker somewhere, but it ended up just being a woman.

That woman.

Bryant stopped dead in his tracks, staring as she loaded wedding presents into a car he didn't recognize. Judging by the two very full trucks in front of her that belonged to his family, those were probably overflow gifts that wouldn't fit into his parent's and brother's vehicles. No doubt they would swing by her place and pick them up the next day.

So that meant that she wasn't just a townsfolk. She was close with his family. They trusted her. Of course, she couldn't only be a friend of Benji's new wife. She had to have ties to everything else too.

That was the issue with a small town. Everything was so incestuously connected. Bryant felt like it was suffocating him.

And yet, he spoke. "Hey."

She jumped, making a startled sound that was far more adorable than it had any right to be. Bryant had enough sense in him to raise both of his hands, although the movement made him lose his balance and totter backward.

She was so *pretty* in the dim lights of the parking lot. He had noticed she was hot before, but this was different. She was softer, sweeter, full of hope and sweet things and all sorts of stuff that weren't in his world.

No wonder she looked down on him. She was like uh... uh... well, he couldn't think of it, but it was some sort of important... thing.

"Don't you know you shouldn't sneak up behind anyone like that! Let alone a woman in the middle of the night?"

"Shouldn't you know not to be out in the wilderness all alone?"

Or at least that was what he thought he said. Judging by the incredibly confused stare she gave him, he guessed that it didn't come out quite right. But what did that matter? He was handsome and rich; he didn't have to talk good.

Except the woman didn't care about that, did she? No, she'd made that abundantly clear. Ugh. He felt himself tipping back towards the downward side of things, coupled with his annoyance that she was ruining his mood without even trying.

"Is being here so painful for you that you have to be inebriated to tolerate it? Or is it just the fact that you're all alone and money makes for a frigid companion?"

Bryant's mind pulled up short at that. Of all the times his family had ever gotten mad at him for getting tipsy, they'd always accused him of needing attention, wanting to make trouble, or having an addiction.

But not *her*. She wanted to know if he was in pain. He was, right? He didn't know. It was so hard to think. Sometimes the stares and disapproval of his family cut him so deeply that he felt as if his soul had welded itself around the wound, refusing for that dagger to ever be removed.

Did she know how they had always disapproved of him? How even when he was young, he could never measure up? How they had compared him and compared him, trying to push him into a mold he didn't fit into, then freezing him out when he refused to comply.

No. She couldn't. She was just a girl.

A woman.

He shook his head. "M'sorry," he managed to get out. "I'll leave you alone."

She didn't want to be near him anyway. He was some degenerate in all these people's eyes. They didn't appreciate his understanding of marketing or social media. His desire to build and create and explore everything life had to offer. They just judged and judged with cold, dead eyes.

When did it get so cold, anyway? And why was it dark?

He took a few steps in a direction that was away from Keiko —although all bets were off if it was the way he was actually supposed to go—but then dizziness swamped him. Usually he could just deep-breathe through such incidents, but before he knew what was happening, he was swaying, and the world was turning sideways.

He didn't hit the ground, however. Instead, small and delicate hands managed to catch him, slowing his momentum enough for him to recover his balance.

Huh. It seemed the woman had caught him. She was so little and waifish. How had she managed to do that?

He opened his mouth to ask her if she was superman, but the words refused to leave his throat. He blinked down at her blearily, sleepiness seeming to coat every cell of his body. As he drifted towards that blissful respite, all he could see were the woman's honeyed brown eyes, the light dusting of freckles across her pale cheeks, and the deep curve in the cupid's bow of her full lips.

She was just so... *beautiful.*

In less than a breath, he decided that he was definitely

going to seduce her. Show her that the stupid, small little world was nothing but a whole bunch of people keeping each other hostage with faux morals.

After all, in the end, he always got what he wanted. He was talented that way.

4

Keiko

For possibly the fifth time in twenty minutes, Keiko carefully walked through the bizarre series of events that had led to her having none other than Bryant Miller —the youngest of the Miller brood—unconscious in her back seat as she drove home.

It certainly wasn't something she had intended. When she had looked out in the reception hall as things were winding down and found him missing, she had been relieved. After so many hours of his gaze boring into her, she'd finally had a shred of privacy.

That, of course, had evaporated when he'd startled her so badly that she'd nearly whipped out the pocketknife in her bra and brandished it at him.

She never used to go around with a weapon, but after everything that had happened with Sophia, she didn't feel comfortable unless she had some way to protect herself. Knives were pretty dangerous, however, and she usually preferred a taser or mace, but neither of those fit into her bridesmaid's dress very well, so blade it was.

A lot of emotions had hit her all at once when she realized who it was and the fact that he was stone-cold drunk. First was fear—was he going to attack her? She had heard such terrible things about how intoxicated people would do things that they wouldn't normally do—mostly from Missy—and almost everyone who knew Bryant didn't speak very highly of him.

But that quickly faded as she took in his body posture and his expression. He wasn't on the attack. If anything, he looked uncertain but eager to please.

Of course, that just made her irritated. Who showed up to their brother's wedding and got so blasted that they were wandering outside completely lost? It was selfish. And *mean*.

So, she'd snapped at him, meaning to embarrass him by showing him how she saw right through him. But the look on his face surprised her, as did his reaction. She expected him to be angry, or his chest to puff out as he got defensive. Instead, he looked surprised. And then... relieved? Almost like he was startled but glad that someone understood him.

That was about the last thing she expected, so when he started to fall, she found herself catching him and helping him back to his feet.

He had been surprisingly muscled under that expensive suit of his. Not that he looked frail, but his build was more like Bradley than his other three brothers. She didn't let herself get distracted, however, and started to move him inside.

Only for him to pass out.

As she drove along, she *knew* she should have taken him home to the Millers—she couldn't find any indication of what hotel he was at on him—but she also knew that he wouldn't like that. That there was some sort of element of pain between him and his family. And, despite his caddishness, she didn't want to subject him to that.

Silly, most definitely, but there was something familiar about whatever it was she felt from him. A sort of ache and un-belonging. Maybe she was projecting, but the haunted look in his eyes was one she had seen in the mirror many times in her slumps.

So, that was how she ended up pulling into her spot in front of her apartment with the prodigal son of the family that had become such a huge part of her life.

Funny how things worked.

But what was decidedly *not* funny was how difficult it was to get him out of the car. He was so *heavy*. Even with her strength from yoga, volunteer work, and martial arts, she struggled just to get him to her door, and she only made it because he was *just* conscious enough to slide his feet for her.

Goodness, what she wouldn't give to be like Missy at the moment. A tall Amazon with biceps on biceps and thighs that could probably crush a watermelon. But she dismissed that thought quickly. She knew one of her biggest triggers was comparing her body to other women.

...but still, it would be *really* convenient to have stronger muscles.

Too bad that she had completely forgotten about the stairs.

"You have *got* to be kidding me," she gasped, feeling sweat build along her neck and trickle down into her pretty dress. She was definitely going to need to get it dry cleaned.

Keiko was aware that most people would give up, or maybe knock on their neighbor's door to ask for help. But she had a stubborn streak just as wide as Dani's, so she took the flight of stairs as a personal challenge. She'd gone through so many incredible challenges; she wasn't going to let a bunch of steps beat her.

So, slight or not, she kicked off her little wedges, threw the shoes up the stairs, then went about climbing them.

It was a struggle, that was for sure, but she did manage to get the two of them stumbling into her apartment, before hauling him over to her small couch.

She had only recently moved out from her parents' home and into Missy's old place. And Keiko had chosen it mostly because of her friend's constant talk about how great the tub was—she was right. As a result, she didn't have much in the way of furniture, but it wasn't like beggars could be choosers. If Bryant wanted a good night's rest on his no-doubt ridiculously expensive and designer couch back at his own penthouse in the city, then he shouldn't have gotten blasted.

Heaving a sigh, she allowed herself exactly one moment to enjoy her victory before moving on. She *definitely* needed some water, which meant Bryant probably did too.

She busied herself with getting them both drinks, along with her small wastebasket from her bathroom in case he got sick. Crossing to him, she saw the man was sitting upright, head tipped back and breathing so deeply that he had to be asleep.

Well, she could rouse him in a few minutes.

Setting the glass down, she went about gathering anything else he might need. A cool washcloth, some dry paper towels, a pillow, and some blankets. Something to soothe his stomach. And a few slices of toast? She'd heard that could help and, although she wasn't sure on it, she figured it couldn't hurt.

She sat across from him in a folding chair that she had "borrowed" from the church, and of course he roused at the smell of the warm bread. Eyes bloodshot, he looked around.

"I don't remember this room," was what she was pretty sure he was saying, although it was somewhat difficult to tell.

"That's because you're in my apartment." She figured she might as well be upfront with him. She didn't want him to think that he was kidnapped or something bizarre like that. Especially since he was so rich that that actually was a real threat for him.

"Oh, yer apartment? Couldn't even wait ta buy me dinner 'for takin' me home?"

Funny. When he was sober he had absolutely no accent, like he had trained it out of himself. But as a drunkard, his accent was about as thick as Pa Miller, who spoke so rarely.

"Don't flatter yourself. This is a kindness because I thought you would not appreciate being carted off to your family's place in your current state."

He grimaced. "Ew, no, I don't wanna."

"Like I said, I surmised as much."

"Surmised?" He chuckled and reached for the water she had left him with a shaky hand. "You're smart, aren't ya?"

"Are you surprised by that?"

"Uh-huh."

Keiko raised her eyebrow, surprised at the frankness. "Why? Because I'm a woman?"

He snorted and gave her a look like that was the most ridiculous thing he had ever heard. "What? No. Lotsa women are smart. Most women, maybe, I think. But no, it's 'cause you're from *here*, and ya run around with my family."

"Ah, and only dumb hicks live in Blackfish County?"

"Ya gotta admit, it is the majority."

Keiko wanted to disagree with him. She knew plenty of good people, but she remembered that she also knew plenty of terrible, selfish, and judgmental people, and trying to argue the thin line with a drunk person was only going to leave her frustrated.

"Whatever you say. Another glass of water?"

"Yeah, I'd like that. Thanks."

She reached for the glass and their hands touched. It was a pretty common occurrence, and not one she felt the need to attribute something to like most romance films, so she just continued as normal.

But that just seemed to boggle Bryant's very drunk mind. "We touched."

"Yes, it happens," she said, standing up to cross to her small kitchen. The apartment wasn't much, but it was hers, and having her own place filled her with a sense of both control and pride. Like she was one step closer to being the healthy, functional Keiko she knew that she could be. "I didn't feel like it was something worth noting."

"You didn't flinch away."

At that she paused and turned to look at him. "Why would I do that?"

"You know," he said, rolling his eyes. "Because I'm a sinner. Dirty. *Unclean*. You've probably heard all about what these hands have done, or where they've been."

He wiggled his eyebrows at that last part, but she didn't miss his tone or expression as the words ticked from his lips. That was self-loathing if she had ever heard it. And a fine bit of rejection too. Resentment. It was almost like listening to Dani or herself speak in high school, all wounded and exhausted, riddled with holes from sharp barbs and the salt of being different rubbed into every mark.

That was a... tortured kind of existence, to say the least. And she was beginning to wonder if maybe Bryant Miller was less of a prodigal son and more of a very hurt, very lost little sheep who thought he was no longer welcome back to the flock.

But that wasn't right at all. There was forgiveness in everything through the Lord. Granted, Bryant had to *ask* for forgiveness first, and that certainly did not seem likely in his current condition.

"So, you normally bring strange guys to yer place a'fer juss meetin' them?" he asked as she came back.

She could tell that he was trying to be playfully flirty, but she wasn't distracted by it.

Had the man ever had a friendly interaction with a woman? Was everything in his world fueled by money or sex? As nice as it could be to be rich—she'd certainly already benefited from the Miller's wealth by proxy—money wasn't enough. The man obviously needed meaningful connections. He needed kindness, and humor, and someone to confide in that had nothing to gain from his fortunes.

What a sad, lonely existence. And with his family harping on him, no wonder he resented them.

"No, I suppose you're an exception."

"Are ya sayin' I'm exceptional?"

She knew that he was expecting her to cut him down. To remind him to be humble. After all, half of what she'd said to him so far had been reproachful. But instead, she nodded.

"Yes, I would say that you are."

He blinked at her owlishly, clearly thrown off whatever drunken continuation of their conversation he had imagined. "What?"

"I said yes, you are exceptional. With a small amount of seed money from selling off your things when your family cut you off, you started a business that is doing well. From what I know, you've managed to invest well, so even if that tanks tomorrow, you'll be set for life."

"...how do you know all that?"

"I've been close to your family for about four years now. I listen, and I remember."

"And you think that's ex-ex-exceptional?"

"Yes. Don't you?"

The man frowned, and she could see his mind behind his eyes sluggishly trying to answer the question. She waited, patiently, as he drained his water then set the glass down.

"It's not enough," he said.

She wasn't sure she heard quite right. "I'm sorry, what was that?"

"It's never enough. I don't think anything... will ever be... enough."

"Enough for what?"

But the man was already asleep, his head tilting down to rest on his chest. She chuckled to herself, then stood once more to put the kettle on. Considering the day she had, some chamomile tea seemed like it was most definitely in order.

She went about making herself a cup, replaying everything in her head that had happened. That's what she usually did when she felt like she had been given a large amount of useful information that needed to be stored for later.

Bryant was nothing like she had imagined. Sure, on the outside he was cocky and licentious and condescending, but she could tell that was a thin blanket to cover some deep-seated issues that reminded her so much of herself. Not that any of that excused his behavior. No, he was still very much responsible for his actions.

But what it did mean was that maybe, just maybe, he didn't

actually want to be the way he was. That he knew there was something better for him but had no idea how to get there.

Or just thought he didn't deserve anything better.

And that spoke to Keiko. She remembered being in times so dark that it seemed there would never be an out. That her life was just torment and pain and the feeling she was never meant for something good. If she didn't have Dani, her parents, and her therapist to help her, she didn't think she would have survived.

Maybe Bryant needed someone like that.

Keiko finished her tea, and a sense of resolve flooded her from her nose to her toes. Purpose—what she had been missing for so long—flooded her and she came to a sudden realization.

She was going to fix Bryant Miller.

5

Bryant

*C*onsciousness was not nice when it smacked Bryant in the face, bringing him from deeply, deeply asleep to awake and uncomfortable in moments flat.

His brain was assaulted by a dozen sensations at once, and he had to sort through them individually before he could go on to do anything else.

For one, his back and neck were throbbing, as if they had spent a night completely unsupported and in an uncomfortable position. For another thing, his head was pounding like someone was banging a mallet against his temple. His tongue was thick and heavy in his mouth, welded in place by just how *dry* it was.

He groaned, about the only sound he could make, and cracked his eyes open. Or at least tried to. They resisted at first, sealed shut with a layer of crust, but his hand sloppily came up to rub them and eventually they were freed.

His vision needed several moments to clear, however, and when it finally did, he was left looking at a place he didn't recognize at all.

...what? This certainly wasn't his hotel. What had happened? Had he finally been kidnapped? Huh, he had insurance for that, but he never thought he'd need to actually use it.

Noises sounded from around a corner, and slowly, Bryant got up to investigate. Every single move felt like torture, but he found that once he got going, it was easier to keep moving.

Eventually, he stumbled into what had to be the tiniest kitchen that he had ever seen. And there, over the very old-looking oven, stood the woman from the wedding, looking completely dressed and put together.

And was she wearing an *apron*? It was such a picture of perfect domesticity that he had to rub his eyes. The woman had no right looking so poised and polished so early on a Sunday morning.

Glancing around, he saw a couple of bags from the local market, which meant she'd already gone out. When he looked to the oven, he saw all the proper fixings for a hangover break-fast including a massive amount of grits.

Why was she being so nice? As his memories trickled back to him, he remembered startling her, then kinda falling over, then them talking and her ignoring all of his advances.

"Why and how are you up so early?" he croaked, his mouth feeling like it was full of sand.

She chuckled at that, reaching into the fridge and grabbing a large bottle of water which she tossed to him. "It's actually after noon. I've already gone to church while you were snooz-ing. It would have been nice to have you there."

His nose wrinkled at that and he busied himself with opening the bottle. But of course, the woman didn't miss that and let out a small laugh.

"Maybe another time then?"

"I wouldn't count on it," he mumbled before chugging the cool liquid.

And goodness, as if it didn't taste *utterly delicious.* He almost didn't come up for air, the refreshment bringing him soothing and coolness that he didn't know he so badly needed.

"I think you would be surprised how life unfolds sometimes," she said.

He opened his mouth to object now that it felt somewhat normal again, but she kept right on talking.

"Why don't you go to the bathroom and freshen up? I'm sure you'd feel better after washing your face and taking a shower."

She was right. He always felt grimy after imbibing too much. "Yeah, okay."

"All the way down the hall. You can't miss it."

He nodded and ducked out, his mind far too full considering how not-quite-awake he was. But as he went through the motions of freshening up, finding the bathroom just as she said he would, more and more from last night came trickling back to him.

But it wasn't until he was splashing cool water on his face that he remembered something in particular.

She'd called him *exceptional.*

Bryant had gotten plenty of compliments in his life, ranging from his looks, to his smarts, to his turn of phrase, but none of them had been from one of the oh-so-pious people of his hometown. And they certainly hadn't been calling him *exceptional.*

What a strange thing to say. What did she even mean by that? She could have been teasing him, but from his memory she seemed fairly earnest.

However... it would do to keep in mind that his memory was formed by his very drunk brain, so he definitely could have misinterpreted things.

Ugh, it was all so confusing, but also intriguing. He wanted to know more about this strange woman and why she did whatever she did. Normally, if a woman had taken him to their place while he was inebriated, he would have expected a good time and skin on skin action. But *she* didn't seem remotely interested in that at all. He was so used to reading people, to knowing exactly what they wanted or expected, that she was throwing him for a loop.

And he couldn't figure out if he liked or hated it.

By the time he finished with cleaning himself up to return to her, she'd finished the meal and had two plates out. One was loaded up in a neat little mountain—which he guessed was his —and the other held a more reasonable amount with fewer foods.

"Not hungry?" he asked, taking the full plate as she handed it to him.

"Lactose intolerant," she said matter-of-factly. "And I'm out of my pills that help me with dairy. I'll get them tomorrow from the pharmacy, but in the meantime, no loaded scrambled eggs or cheesy potatoes for me."

But if that was the case, that meant that she had made them just for him.

He had no idea what to think about all that.

Nevertheless, he followed her back to the small living room that he had woken up in. She gestured for him to sit on her couch while she gracefully settled onto one of those metal folding chairs. Where was this girl's furniture?

He had no idea, but she didn't seem to catch onto his bewilderment. Instead, she balanced her plate on her knees and leaned forward to unfold a part of the coffee table, working the metal posts attached to it until it made a solid, if not slightly wobbly, surface for them to eat on.

She put her plate on it like the whole thing was completely normal. He couldn't help but wonder if this was what his parents meant when they said he had no idea how some people struggled.

Bryant followed her lead, but his trepidation quickly faded as he dug into the food. The meal was good and hit his churning stomach just right. For being such a thin girl, she certainly knew how to cook.

"So was this your plan?"

"Pardon?" she asked around the toast that she was very carefully chewing.

"Get me to your house and show me what a great housewife you could be? I have to say, it's pretty unorthodox, but I'm impressed."

She smiled thinly. Not in an irritated way, just in a way that said she saw through him and found his attempt so flimsy that it was amusing.

She finished chewing. "Tell me, is it exhausting thinking you're the center of the universe, or is that just how you get through the day?"

Ouch. All right, so it probably wasn't an elaborate scheme to win his affection. That was too bad. It certainly would make his plan easier to accomplish.

Then again, he probably wouldn't be interested if she was easy to figure out. In fact, he was pretty sure that he remembered thinking that he was going to seduce her. Not a bad idea, actually.

"So I'll take that as a no."

"Yes, that and the meal are the only things you'll be taking from here."

Yeowch. There was steel to that comment. Bryant wished he could banter with her because he knew it would be fun, but his brain was still recovering from his hangover and his body felt sluggish. Next time he met her, he would need to make sure he was on his A-game.

That is, if they did meet again.

For the first time in his life, Bryant was looking at the fact that he might fail irreparably right out the gate. That rarely happened to him, but he had a feeling that their interaction happening when he was literally drunk off his feet had damaged things pretty heavily.

They continued eating, and he tried idle conversation a few times, but every time he got flirty, she would politely shut him down. After the third time, he figured three strikes and he was out, so he stopped. It was one thing to pursue a woman; it was another to harass her to the point of annoyance. Besides, she had already taken him in and helped him instead of ditching him on his family—who would no doubt use it as a chance to preach to him again about the dangerous path he was going down—so she deserved not to be hassled in her own home.

So eventually, when the meal ended and she put the dishes in the sink, he took that as his cue to leave. He called a cab and went about righting the cushions on the couch and asking her if she needed any help.

Of course, she politely declined, and he was left with nothing to do but wait awkwardly. After a long moment's hesitation, he decided to take a risk.

"Hey, I appreciate what you did for me. Maybe I could grab your number and take you out some time as a thank-you?"

He fully expected her to say no, and as much as it would sear his pride, he would respect that. His family may have thought he was scum, but he respected a woman's right to say no for whatever reason she wanted. It wasn't like he had exactly presented himself in the best light.

"Aren't you supposed to ask for my name first?"

What? Her name? Had he really not... with a blush, he realized that he hadn't. She knew who he was, but he literally knew nothing of her.

"Oh, uh, yes. Please. What is your name?"

"Keiko. Keiko Albryte. Nice to meet you, Bryant Miller."

She extended her hand, and once more he found himself touching her. Her fingers were small and delicate compared to his, and her skin was sinfully smooth. He wanted to let the touch linger, but he wanted to not be an even bigger creep, so he quickly let go.

"I guess I'm going about this all out of order."

"Yes, but I'm guessing that you usually like to forge your own path."

"Eh, that might have a ring of truth to it."

She let out a dry chuckle but then moved to do nothing else. Bryant guessed that was her way of politely refusing the number question, but some part of him wanted to be sure.

"I'm guessing it's the same area code as all my brothers?"

She said nothing, her brown eyes staring him down inscrutably. But after a moment of looking him over, she nodded slowly and held her hand out. He stared at her, confused, before realizing that she wanted his phone.

He pulled it from his pocket, relieved to see it was alive and still on its last ten percent. Quickly, she typed up a new contact, and then he was surprised when she called it.

He heard the telltale buzz of a phone vibrating on the kitchen counter, and she smiled.

"There, now I have your number too."

"Uh, thanks," he said, taking his phone back and feeling entirely off-balance. It wasn't normal for him to be anything less than sure-footed, but he was liking the adrenaline rush it was bringing. "I'll see you around."

"Yes, I believe that you will."

6

Keiko

"*S*ushi platter for two?"

Keiko nodded, eager to put food in her stomach after what felt like a long day of work, even though it had really been just a five-hour shift. Still, her stomach had been too upset that morning to put anything into it, so now it was massively upset with her for getting off her eating schedule. One of the things that helped her stay steady and healthy was having regimens.

Oh, well. She felt like she was in a good enough position to roll with it, and it certainly helped that Sophia was tearing through their just-delivered food ravenously right across from her.

They were an unlikely pair. While she liked the very young woman, she'd known her the least of any of her circle and was surprised Sophia was comfortable with her. Granted, their hanging out was mostly due to convenient circumstance rather than anything else.

Keiko worked in the city library every Monday, Wednesday, and Friday from eleven to three. It wasn't enough to fully support her, but it helped supplement the stipend the church gave her, which was largely what had allowed her to live on her own. Of course, being in the city during those times lined up very well with Sophia's therapy visits. The young woman was seeing someone who specifically worked with people suffering from abuse and all the trauma that went with it, and she went twice a week.

Of course, her therapy didn't last five hours, so once her appointment was done—or on Fridays when she didn't have therapy at all—she would either take a cab or ride-share to the library and study on the computers in a GED certification program. Then, once Keiko clocked out, they would go get a very late lunch/early dinner.

Which was exactly how they ended up at her favorite sushi place together, Sophia forking down food like she was afraid it would disappear.

"Hey, didn't you and your therapist talk about that?"

The young woman stopped, looking at Keiko sheepishly. "Right. No one is going to steal it. And I don't have to be on the lookout."

Keiko smiled and picked up her own set of chopsticks. She had been quite pleased when she had been the first person to introduce Sophia to sushi—and the slender woman had loved it. Perhaps it was surprisingly stereotypical for Keiko to like it so much, being half Japanese and all, but it was what it was.

"Eating slowly is hard when the food's so delicious, isn't it?" Keiko said, eyes crinkling.

"Yeah, it is."

To be truthful, Keiko would never have been able to afford the fancy lunches they had—especially considering how much Sophia could eat—if Bradley didn't end up paying for it. She felt a bit guilty, relying on the credit card he gave to Sophia, but he had expressed to Keiko nearly a dozen times how grateful he was for her trips to the city with Sophia.

She knew that, in truth, Bradley could come with her himself; he would move heaven and earth for the recovering girl. But Sophia's therapist had recommended that Sophia not rely on only him and that having other friends help and support her would be much healthier. So, their little lunch dates stayed.

Normally, they kept their conversation pretty Sophia-focused, talking about what she had learned in therapy, or her progress on her GED or anything else she'd learned. But Keiko was itching to talk to *someone* about her plan. Normally she would lean on Dani, who would no doubt sarcastically pick apart everything in the best way possible. But Keiko wasn't about to text Dani while she was on her honeymoon.

"You're quiet," Sophia remarked around a mouthful of *unagi.*

"Am I?" Keiko mused, dipping her piece of *tomago* sushi in soy sauce then putting a tiny piece of ginger on top.

"Yeah, normally you'd be asking about what I've learned today, or something teacherly like that."

"I guess I've got a lot on my mind."

"Really?" Sophia swallowed then moved her empty glass to the edge of the table for a refill. "Then why don't you talk to me for once. Friendships are supposed to be a give and take, so lemme take a little." Her nose scrunched up. "All right, that didn't exactly come out right, but you know what I mean."

Keiko couldn't help but chuckle. "It sounds like *you* have something particular on your mind."

The young Latina blushed so furiously that her tanned skin turned bright red. "I-I-I mean, can you blame me? I am an engaged woman, after all. And my fiancé..." She huffed out a breath, and it was the most infatuated that Keiko had ever seen Sophia look. "He's pretty hot. And nice. I mean... like the nicest guy I ever met. And *smart* too. He's been helping me with a bunch of math, and he's practically a genius."

It wasn't often that Keiko ever heard Sophia say so much at once, and even rarer that she looked so dreamy-eyed and head over heels. The look was good on her, one full of hope and happiness, and Keiko couldn't help but wonder what it would feel like to be that in love.

She didn't even know if she had that capacity within her.

"Look at you," Sophia said, shaking her head. "Got me talking about myself again. Just dish before I embarrass myself further."

"All right," Keiko said slowly, trying to gather her thoughts. "You know of Bryant Miller, correct?"

"Who doesn't?" she said with a snort, sinking down into her oversized hoody. If there was one thing Sophia hadn't quite been able to shake, it was her penchant for oversized clothing. "Kinda the bad boy of the bunch. A black sheep if you will."

"Apt enough. Well, did you notice at the wedding he got somewhat... inebriated?"

"That's a nice way of putting it. With how Ben was complaining on the ride home, you'd think he was absolutely plastered. Where did he even go off too?"

"That's the thing... where he got off to was my place."

Sophia's chopsticks fell to the table with a clatter. "Ms. Keiko Ann Albryte, did you sleep with Bryant Miller?"

She practically yelled it, and Keiko had to lean over the table to press her hand to the girl's mouth. She realized too late that probably wasn't the best thing to do to a woman recovering from domestic abuse.

"How do you even know my full na—"

Unsurprisingly, Sophia knocked her hand away. "Don't touch me without my permission."

"Right, right. I'm sorry. That was wrong of me. I panicked. But no, I did not sleep with Bryant Miller."

The girl deflated. "Sorry, I just… with what I know of you, and what I'd heard of him, that just seemed like the most impossible thing I ever heard. I wouldn't judge you if you did, you know. I don't think I should be judgin' much of anybody considering…" She trailed off, biting her lip as she did.

Keiko reached out to her, but this time she waited for Sophia to give her a nod before curling their hands together.

"You have nothing to be ashamed of. You stood up to him, and you're in the process of taking him to court. I'm sure you're going to help a whole lot of other women with your case."

"Yeah, uh, you're right." She took a deep breath and returned to her plate. "So, you just happened to take a very drunk Bryant Miller to your place. And then… what? You had a Bible study."

Keiko chuckled at that. She could almost see the handsome man hissing at a Bible like a snake. "I don't think he's quite ready for that yet."

"Yet?"

Goodness, Sophia was so sharp.

"Yes, yet. But I do think, after spending a good bit of time with him, that I might be able to… shepherd him onto the path, let's say."

"Really?" Sophia asked dubiously. "Isn't this the guy who's

been ostracized by his family for nine years? And rather than asking for forgiveness, built his own gambling and liquor company just to piss them off?"

"I actually don't think he did it just to anger them. It's... complicated, I guess. But I think this rift between him and his family started long, long ago. Before he ever left the ranch for college. I think if I give him coping mechanisms and strategies, and maybe some ways to open up lines of communication, he might be able to heal. Maybe even the Miller family could become whole again."

"Really? You think you can do all that?"

Keiko shrugged. "You know what it's like to be wandering alone and lost in this world. Sometimes it just takes one kind act to show you that an entirely different reality is there. One where people have open hearts and kindness fuels things instead of greed."

Sophia smiled softly, and Keiko could just imagine what the previously abused woman was remembering. "I... I guess that has happened to me. And to Missy too. Actually, it's kinda happened to all of us, hasn't it?"

Keiko nodded. "I was so very lucky my parents noticed that I was spiraling out of control and got me the tools I needed to survive. If I can give Bryant those tools too, or at least nudge him in the direction of finding those tools, I think that would be worthwhile, would it not?"

"It would." Sophia picked up another piece of sushi and popped it into her mouth whole. She chewed for a while, clearly thinking, before she finally spoke again. "Isn't that kinda like playing God though?"

Keiko shook her head. "No, playing God would be judging him. Trying to force him to change. Believe it or not, I think that's been a huge part of the problem. Too many Christians he's interacted with, too many people who are close to him, have handed down judgment and told him he's bad. And if enough people tell you you're wicked-bad-wrong, why even try to be good?

"That's what I think this is all about. He just needs to be shown that he's not this corrupted thing, and that he has choices. And I'm well aware that he could choose to keep on doing what he's doing, but... I just have this *feeling*. Sometimes, when he talked to me, there was this deep, *deep* pain there. And pain wants to be healed."

"I mean, you definitely have a point. And Keiko, I know you're probably the smartest out of all of us—except maybe Bradley—but are you sure this is a trouble you want to take on? I know you've counseled a whole lot of people, but are you qualified to 'fix' someone who has such a deep wound? What if you make it worse? I like ya a whole lot, but being insightful is not the same as being a therapist."

Keiko's knee-jerk reaction was to insist that it would be fine, but she realized that Sophia had a very valid point. She was attempting to help someone with what she perceived to be some pretty severe emotional damage. She wasn't certified. She wasn't licensed. There was a difference between being a good friend and shepherd to someone and stepping dangerously out of bounds.

"Those are good questions. I'll have to think on that."

"Huh, uh, okay."

"Why do you sound surprised?"

Sophia shrugged and continued to eat her sushi for a few moments before confessing. "I just, uh... hearing that from someone as smart as you is, uh, it's nice. That's all."

Keiko smiled softly. "You're not stupid, Sophia. I hope you know that."

"It's a work in progress," she admitted.

Now if anything, Keiko understood that. Grabbing another piece of sushi, she raised it as if they were about to toast. "To progress then."

Sophia smiled brightly and picked up her own piece. "To progress!"

The rest of their meal sank into a much less serious conversation, and about an hour or so later, they were headed out into Keiko's junky car and driving back home.

Right after she had dropped Sophia off, and before she'd even started for home, her phone buzzed. Looking at it, she was surprised to see that it was none other than Bryant himself. She hadn't exactly had a ton of time to think over Sophia's words, but she found herself opening the text anyway.

HEY, just wanted to check in and ask about that dinner I owe you for not ditching me on my family. Are you free tomorrow?

KEIKO SAT THERE for far too long, and if any of the Millers looked out their window, they were probably wondering what she was doing. But, before she really thought it through, she went ahead and replied.

YES. What do you have in mind?

7

Bryant

*B*ryant rehearsed another greeting as he drove to pick up Keiko, his nerves bunching up in a way he wasn't used to. Normally he was pretty busy during the week, dedicating himself to his job and growing his brand, but that was only because that was basically his entire life and he had maybe one or two control issues.

But currently, Keiko seemed like a good enough reason to take a day off and let all of his employees, that he paid so much money to, work for him.

All he needed to do was get her to loosen up and get a little taste of adrenaline. If there was one thing that he had learned about uptight, small-town girls, it was that they really just wanted to break all the rules holding them back and be free. Getting them there just took a catalyst. And he was more than happy to do that.

He arrived in front of her place then texted her, and less than a few moments later, Keiko emerged. She was dressed in an oversized, gray sweater and dark green leggings, casual, just like he had advised.

But even though her outfit wasn't inherently sexy, she certainly looked quite attractive. Her long, dark brown hair was done up in a bun on her head, and her face was fresh and clean. She crossed to his car gracefully, opening the passenger's side and sliding in.

"So, are you going to tell me what we're doing now?"

Bryant shook his head. "It's a surprise. We're going to the city, and that's all you need to know."

"Huh, that almost sounds like I'm being kidnapped."

He made a dramatic sound. "You wound me with such distrust."

"Really?" she quipped right back. "Because I have a feeling, in your line of work, it takes so much more to get under your skin."

He chuckled at that. He wasn't used to someone going toe-to-toe with him so quickly. Some of his board did, especially his CFO, but that had taken a couple of years to build up. But Keiko was fearless, in a way. Able to look right through him and his bluster in an instant.

"I suppose that might have a hint of truth to it."

"I know. That's why I said it."

He chuckled, then pulled away from the curb. It was an hour drive to the city, so they certainly were going to have plenty of time to talk.

Which was good, because he wanted to get to know the woman who seemed to have caught his attention. Maybe if he could just puzzle her out, he wouldn't be so obsessed with her and could get back to his regular ol' life.

"So, where did you go to college?"

He was surprised when she was the one who spoke first. He answered, and soon they sank into an entirely banal conversation full of factoids that seemed important to know but didn't really help him *learn* about Keiko.

Apparently, she went to the community college in the city to get a BA in library sciences, and that was how she got her job in said city's library. She—unsurprisingly—also worked with the church quite often. Running Bible studies, the welcoming committee, the reception set up, it kind of went on and on.

She still asked where they were going several more times, and he could see her trying to figure it out, but she definitely had no idea.

He couldn't wait to see her face when they pulled into their destination. He built up a whole reaction in his head, but when he turned into the parking lot of the paintball shooting range he had picked out, Keiko looked only mildly interested.

Huh, that was disappointing.

He wondered if she just didn't know where they were, but when he parked, she got right out of the car and looked around.

"Huh, I've never played paintball before," she murmured.

All right, so she definitely knew where they were. Hmm. It seemed she really was unruffle-able, which was somewhere between impressive and irritating.

But that was fine. Maybe she was just keeping cool. The real fun part would be once they got inside and got started.

Bryant fully expected to spend most of his time protecting her. He didn't want her to get *hurt*; he just wanted her to get excited about the *possibility* of being hurt. There was nothing like a good chemical thrill to get the blood pumping, and when the blood was pumping, people were more likely to do rash things.

Huh... when his mind phrased it like that, it almost sounded like he was trying to take advantage of her.

But that was nonsense because he definitely wasn't.

All smiles, he went about buying them a full package, which included rental armor and a lesson from one of the workers there. To her credit, Keiko took it all in stride, nodding along like she understood, which only built up the anticipation inside of him.

"Don't worry," he said as an employee led them to one side of the obstacle course with some other random people who would be on their team. "I'll watch out for you."

"Oh?" she said, smiling blithely at him. "What makes you think I'm worried?"

He opened his mouth—no doubt to say something that wasn't nearly as clever—but he was interrupted as their instructor started telling them how the game would start and a few more rules.

Number one, no headshots. Number two, no parkour. Rule three, no poor sportsmanship.

It went on from there, but Bryant had come to this place plenty of times so he tuned it out, instead watching Keiko's face.

He wondered just how good she was at holding a poker face, because all she seemed was mildly curious. Her paintball gun hung at her side, and her posture was relaxed.

Maybe she just didn't understand how a paintball fight went? It was plenty exhilarating once the pellets started flying and people were running every which way. Yeah, he could see it now, her standing there, wide-eyed and in wonder as he took out several guys who swarmed her.

...except that was really cheesy and he had never been that lame.

He was so preoccupied with his thoughts that he was startled when the buzzer to start the round went off. Everyone on his team ran every which direction, except for Keiko, who casually strolled to the side.

"What, where are you going?" Bryant asked, trailing after her. So far, this date wasn't going anything like he'd imagined. Instead of all adrenaline and excitement, she was acting as if she was purse shopping or something equally banal.

"I saw a nice shed from the main building when we were getting equipped. It looked like a nice spot."

"A nice spot for what?" he asked.

She looked to him with an expression that he absolutely could not interpret. "You'll see."

Instantly his eyes went to her lips, and his mind jumped to kissing them while pressing her against the tin wall of whatever paintball shed she was talking about. It would be something, to cage her small body between his thick arms, her looking up at him with want and desire while—

"Yes, this will do."

He shook his head to free himself from the fantasy just in time to see Keiko shift her gun strap so it hung over her back, and then she *climbed the wall of the shack.*

"What are you doing?" he asked, running up after her. Except he was standing on the ground as she clambered onto the roof, adjusting herself and her gun once she was in a standing position.

"Finding a vantage point. You'd be surprised how often people never look *up*."

He wanted to ask how she knew that, but then she was bringing her gun's scope up to her eye and then squeezing the trigger. The sound of three balls being released cracked through the air, and the next thing he knew he heard loud curses and a cry of "where did that come from?"

"You did not just shoot three people from up there," he said, completely bewildered.

"Just two," she said, adjusting quickly and firing another set of shots. "I missed one. He seems experienced. I think I'll take him out next."

"Take him out? What are—"

But she was already *jumping* off the roof, landing in a crouch and rolling forward until she hopped up onto her feet like it was nothing. She looked back to him, a serene expression on her face.

"If you say any comments that relate to 'ninja' in any way, shape, or form, I will shoot you in the head with my bright pink pellets."

Bryant swallowed, feeling his body react to this woman in a way that was almost embarrassing. "That's against the rules."

"Oh, is it?" she fluttered her eyelashes at him and if that didn't just make his heart jump. "I guess I wasn't listening. Now come on."

Who *was* this woman?

He had no answer, and he found himself watching in awe as she calmly walked around several bales of hay, then some planks, before going up close to one and leveling her gun.

Three more shots and then more cursing, and Bryant belatedly saw someone stomping off the field.

"Do you think it would be poor sportsmanship to take them all out?"

"All who?"

"The other team."

"Keiko, there's no way you can—"

"Duck."

He didn't know what drove him to obey her as soon as the words left her mouth, but he did. The next thing he knew there was the sound of hay crunching above his head, the pop of a gun, then the sharp snap of a paintball hitting armor.

"Dude, that was insane. Good shot."

Bryant looked over his shoulder to see a large man standing on top of the hay bale, nodding his head appreciatively even though he was out.

"Thank you," Keiko answered before looking to Bryant. "You bought us a three-game package, right?"

He could only nod as he got back up to his feet. "There's usually more people as we get later into the afternoon."

"All right, I'll stop for now then. I'll have my fun when there's more people for everyone."

And without another word, she walked over to the sidelines and sat down.

"Really?" Bryant asked, so surprised by the turn in events that he didn't know what was up and what was down. "Just like that?"

"You heard the rules. Poor sportsmanship is frowned upon here. Taking out an entire team of people in five minutes who just came here to enjoy themselves doesn't sound like good sportsmanship." She waved her hand at him. "Now go, enjoy yourself and bag a few hits of your own."

He wanted to argue with her, he really did, but she was already laying back on her elbows with her gaze on the sky, a blissful expression on her face.

Bryant was beginning to get the feeling that he was completely out of his league.

TRUE TO HER WORD, Keiko really did wait until the later afternoon matches to actually *try*, and boy was she something.

She wasn't infallible, especially once the employees started playing, but dang if she wasn't unnervingly good. By the time their full package was over, Bryant had been hit a handful of times, almost all in spots around his armor, while Keiko had taken a grand total of three shots. When everyone was filing out, he even overheard a couple of the other team bragging about how they'd managed to get a hit on her.

And it was indeed a bragging right, because Bryant had been next to her the whole time as she'd calmly taken shot after shot after shot, cutting across the field and using the terrain to her advantage without even ending up breathing hard.

Somehow, he managed to wait until they were all the way in his car before turning to her with a mix of wonder and shock. "What just happened in there?"

She blinked at him, looking happy and sated like she had just enjoyed a good movie rather than trouncing a good amount of people at a game they were very good at. "What do you mean?"

He narrowed his gaze at her. "You know exactly what I mean."

Surprisingly, a soft laugh left her mouth. "I do. It's nothing that exciting, really. My father wanted me to be able to provide for myself if I was ever in a bad situation or if there was some sort of national emergency. I've been hunting and handling different rifles of his since I was eight years old. Once I was a teenager, he got me used to other types of guns at the shooting range. They were never much my thing, but I still appreciate the knowledge. Especially since it turns out that the paintball rifle isn't that much different."

Bryant couldn't believe it. A lot of the things that he had assumed about Keiko were very suddenly being proven wrong, and he didn't know what to think of it. He was frustrated that she defied his ability to figure her out when his "thing" was understanding and schmoozing people, but he was also incredibly intrigued. What gave her the right to be so... so... *unpredictable.*

"Well, you certainly have talent."

"Thank you. I appreciate that. Although, I do wonder why you even brought me here. I take it by your question and the look on your face that you didn't know about my affinity for guns, so that does leave your purpose in question."

There she went again, seeing through him like he was cellophane. Normal people didn't do that, and yet she said it so flippantly, like it was just a thought off the top of her head.

He had to say *something* however, so he decided to go with mostly the truth. "Honestly, I thought that maybe you might be a little... uptight, and some adrenaline could let me know the real you."

"Ah, that is a classic strategy. Fear and excitement are powerful bonding emotions."

"Yeah, bonding emotions."

He pulled out of the parking lot and once again, he found he had no idea how to drive their conversation. But instead of stressing him out. It was almost... nice? Often when he was talking to people, he felt like they were working through a script that he had been able to read way beforehand. Usually, nothing surprised him and everything was predictable. But with Keiko, it was like he was experiencing everything for the first time. It was chaos, but it was fun. He found it challenging.

And sure enough, she continued to surprise him by starting up a conversation with him on her own, talking about fun or exciting things that she had noticed on the paintball battlefield. It was through her little stories and factoids that he realized that she did indeed have a good time. And, although the little outing didn't go exactly how he had planned, he found his chest swelling with pride that she enjoyed herself. For some reason, it felt like an accomplishment.

By the time they got to her apartment building, the conversation was winding down, but he found himself not wanting it to end. He didn't want to go to his penthouse in the city and spend the night alone, facing the no-doubt hundreds of work emails and new business propositions that were waiting in his inbox.

His mind rattled through a dozen or so excuses to extend their time together before he finally settled on one.

"You know, with as good as you are, don't you think it's a little mean how much you let me get hit?" He gave her a wounded look. "I'm gonna have some real welts and bruises tomorrow."

She gave him a look that he began to recognize as her being mischievous. On anyone else, it would be a sort of pleasant grin, but he was beginning to understand all those little microexpressions on that pretty face of hers.

"I'm sorry, am I misremembering it, or were your exact words 'I'll watch out for you'? That doesn't imply that you need to be babysat."

"Babysat? *Ow.*"

She just shrugged, not looking even the slightest bit guilty and stepped out of the car. Bryant was disappointed that it hadn't worked, and they indeed were going to part, but that feeling quickly faded as she leaned back into his open window.

"Well, aren't you coming?"

"Huh?"

She gave him a serious look. "If you're going to try to guilt me about your oh-so-egregious boo-boos, you should really work on your follow-up. Come in, and I'll give you some witch hazel and vitamin E oil to put on them."

"Oh, witch hazel? I'm not sure what the big man upstairs will think about that."

"Funny, I would have thought you'd be all about anything that the 'big man' doesn't like."

"Come now, that makes me sound predictable."

"And you aren't?"

"*Ouch.* That hurts worse than the bruises."

"I'm not surprised. They do say that a rich man's ego is his most fragile point."

Bryant laughed, putting the car into park and getting out. "You know, with the way you're tearing me down, I'd almost think you didn't like me."

"And by the way you're smiling, I'd almost think you like it when I bring you down to earth a little."

"Oh, is that what you're doing?"

She shrugged and led him inside. Strange to think the last time he had gone into her apartment he had been drunk off his feet, because he was noticing all sorts of things about it.

It wasn't that it was a slum, but it was just so... so... *old.* There was a sagging sort of oldness to it and everything was so closed-in. Her place was nothing like the ranch, which was sprawling and open and free. Sometimes, when he was particularly exhausted from the coldness and bustle of the city, he would wish he could go back home.

But the issue was that going home inevitably meant running into his family. Even the last couple of times he had visited just to see the horses and check in on Bart had ended up with terse or uncomfortable conversations.

Ugh.

"Stay here, I'll go get what you need from the bathroom."

Bryant nodded and sat down on her couch while she went off. But he grew antsy too soon, his adrenaline from the exciting paintball session still coursing through him.

He would normally poke around, snoop nosily at any pictures or personal effects, but Keiko's apartment was bare. He decided she must have moved in fairly recently, because it didn't seem lived in at all. The only room that seemed remotely habituated was the bathroom with its old and impressive claw-foot tub.

So, it was while he was sitting there, twiddling his thumbs, that an idea came to him. Some people might think it was mean, and it certainly wasn't polite, but it was so perfect that the next thing he knew, he was standing up and pulling his shirt off.

While he wasn't nearly as jacked as his brothers—especially Bart, who was basically just a mountain of muscle the last time he saw him—he did spend plenty of time in the gym to keep himself fit. Being in top shape was a point of vanity, for the most part. His brothers all stayed strong and powerful as a result of their work on the ranch. The last thing he wanted was to look scrawny next to all of them and give them another reason to look down on him.

He smiled to himself as he turned to face the corner that Keiko would no doubt be rounding at any moment. He could see the moment in his head now. It was easy to deny attraction and handwave away temptation when everyone was fully clothed. But he'd learned that showing some skin could go a long way in the game of seduction.

And... it was kind of strange, but he wanted Keiko to *want* him. He'd had plenty of trysts and girlfriends and lovers, but he had always been confident that they definitely wanted him. But with Keiko, she reacted as if he was just another, everyday person and not a handsome billionaire who had been on about a dozen magazine covers.

Her lack of interest hurt his pride just as much as it challenged him, which he knew was strange, but he didn't feel like questioning it.

Sure enough, he heard Keiko's steps around the corner and then she was in the living room. She was already prattling out directions when her eyes landed on his torso, and suddenly several things happened at once.

She let out that same adorably startled sound that she had made that night at the wedding and everything fell from her hands. Her eyes went wide and one of her hands went to her mouth.

Finally, he got the reaction he had been hoping for.

Taking a step towards her, he sent her his most charming smile. He wanted her to know that he would take care of her. That he would treat her right and make sure she left the experience happy, sated, and maybe with some nicer furniture.

Slowly, he bent to pick up the items that she had dropped, standing up and closing the remaining distance between them to place them back in her hands.

"Well, aren't you going to take care of me?" He said as he gently tucked a strand of hair behind her ear. He couldn't help but wonder if anyone had ever held her tenderly. Showed her that she was desirable and admirable and worthy of so much magic.

She stared at him for a long moment, almost too long, the tension mounting between them. Bryant wondered if he should just kiss her, but she hadn't spoken yet, and he always liked to make sure that his partners were one hundred percent on board and into what was happening.

Then, just as suddenly as the whole thing had happened,

the moment broke. Letting out a strangled sort of gasp, she shoved the items back in his hand and took several large steps back.

"You need to go."

Very abruptly, Bryant realized he had somehow made a grave misstep. Confusion swirling through him, he stood there for a moment, surprised.

"I said *go!* I need you to leave *right now!*"

Right. If she wanted him out of her house, he needed to get out. Grabbing his shirt, he hurried out, wondering what had just happened and how Keiko just turned everything he knew on its head.

Not for the first time, he was pretty sure that he had just ruined everything.

8

Keiko

*K*eiko wondered if she was in over her head.

When she had imagined what it would be like to bring the errant Miller son back into the fold, it hadn't involved seeing him shirtless or having him be so charming and humble. But that was exactly what had happened, and her mind kept flashing to that fateful moment.

She'd come around the corner, and he had just been *there*.

He wasn't as tanned as his brothers, or as big, but that didn't mean he wasn't absolutely striking. Keiko could see every cut of his muscles, every rippling striation as he breathed, and even a small appendectomy scar low down on his belly.

He was a dream, and she knew that many people would have welcomed with open arms what he was offering. But what she was completely surprised by was how much she wanted to reach out and touch him. To *feel* exactly what Bryant Miller was all about.

She wasn't going to lie; the sensation had her shaken. She wasn't a nun, by any means, but she'd never been so viscerally attracted to a man like *that*. It was as if the entire world had vanished in a puff of smoke, leaving just the two of them.

Temptation had slid along her tongue and trickled down her throat like honey. But she clamped down on that hard and barely managed to yell at him to get out.

...but would she have done anything if he hadn't? She didn't know, and that upset her more than she liked to admit.

She trudged through her weekly tasks but received no satisfaction from the routine. She was distracted, frustrated. She tried her best to keep it together, but as her confidence in herself flagged, she grew more and more restless.

It didn't help that every time she closed her eyes, Bryant was there.

She didn't like that. She didn't want to be one of his thralls, all caught up in the flesh and desire and forgetting about the things that mattered, about the eternal things. By the time Thursday rolled around, she was a right mess and decided some time on the ranch would help her.

Normally, she would go to Dani's and they'd ride some horses around. Her family had an especially old and gentle horse who was perfect for a leisurely trot, that had always liked Keiko. But Dani was still on her month-long honeymoon, which meant that the Miller ranch was the more viable option.

Maybe, if she was lucky, she would find Missy there in the stalls. She didn't muckrake nearly as much as she used to considering she had her own rescue business now, but she would still lend a hand from time to time.

Nodding to herself, Keiko got into her car and headed over.

She knew she should probably text first, but chances that Missy had her phone on her and was getting a signal were few and far between. Besides, if the Amazon-like woman wasn't there, there was still a chance Chasity, Sophia, or even one of the boys would be willing to show her around.

She made it to the ranch in record time—not that she was trying to. She guessed that subconsciously she just wanted to get there as soon as possible. When she arrived, she parked in the little dirt lot for the workers that came from town then headed towards the barn.

Sure enough, Missy was there, but she wasn't raking out one of the stalls. Instead, she was standing beside a stack of carriers, letting the inhabitants out one by one.

"What are you doing?" Keiko asked curiously, coming up behind Missy as she gave the cat she was releasing a treat, then watched it slink off into the deeper parts of the barn.

"Just bringing some of the barn cats home. They've all had a good recovery."

"Were they sick?"

She shook her head. "No, they were having so many kittens that it was getting to be too much, and some of the girls were starting to have more and more rejections. I fixed about five of them and have been taking care of them for the past week. I'm letting them out now, and then I'm going to see if I can round up a new crew."

"Wow, I didn't realize there were so many here," Keiko said, coming up alongside the carriers.

She had expected the felines to be on edge, as cats often were when they were carted anywhere, but all of them seemed relaxed enough. Missy really did seem to have a way with creatures. Keiko wished she could say the same, but unfortunately most animals seemed to find her decidedly average.

Except for that one horse on Dani's farm, of course. He was the best.

"Well, they're not *all* in this barn. They go out in the fields to hang with the horses. All in all, I'd say there's maybe fifty or so in our area, but that number's been climbing since I've come here and gotten them all flea and worm medication, so now I gotta make sure they don't overpopulate."

"Fifty, that seems like a lot to take care of."

"Well, I'm not going to fix *every* cat. I just don't think that's possible. But I'm definitely getting all of the older girls who are getting worn out, and most of the tomcats. Did you know a cat can get pregnant even while they're nursing?"

"Uh, no, I didn't actually. That seems very exhausting. I'm grateful I'm not a cat."

"Right? The always-landing-on-your-feet thing is nice, but I'm not sure it's worth it." The blond chuckled, and she finally looked to Keiko. "So, what brings you here? I rarely see you out of town without Dani. You missing the ranch life with her being gone so long?"

"Maybe," Keiko admitted. "Do you have any really nice horses that don't mind an inexperienced rider? I thought it'd be nice to just trot through a field or something like that."

"You know what? I think I have a horse in mind. It's the one that Bradley used with Sophia. I think he's up in his office. I'm just gonna grab him and go check."

Keiko flushed at that. As much as she enjoyed helping others, she loathed feeling like a burden. She was so used to being independent that way.

"Oh, you don't have to. I would hate to be a bother."

Missy leveled her with a look that Keiko had seen stop Bart right in his tracks when he was about to go into a manic rant.

"Please girl, you are family here. It'll only take a second, and we can both see if Ma made up some fresh lemonade."

"I... all right. If you insist."

"Funny story, I just about insist on everything."

Keiko chuckled at that. Missy's strong nature was almost as notorious as Dani's, but she admired both of the women for that. It had taken her so long to stand up for herself, but that just seemed to come to both women naturally.

"So I've noticed."

They headed inside where there indeed was a fresh pitcher of lemonade. Keiko busied herself with pouring a glass for her and Missy each—she was familiar enough with the Miller kitchen to help herself—and waited for the blond to go all the way up to Bradley's office.

Keiko realized she had never been up in that room. Probably because it seemed like Sophia and Bradley's little haven where they both escaped from everything to just be together.

Once more, she felt a strange sort of shift in her belly, a sort of longing for that, but she quickly dismissed it.

And she dismissed it just in time, as both Sophia and Missy came stampeding down the stairs, with Bradley in tow.

"I hear you want to go out on a ride?"

Keiko nodded. "I thought it might be nice. I feel like I've been cooped up for too long."

"You know, the weather is beautiful today. I think we could all use an outing." Bradley said, crossing to the fridge and grabbing a water bottle.

"Oh, really?" That surprised Keiko. As far as she knew, the only thing that could usually tear Bradley away from his work was Sophia herself. Interesting. Maybe they both were growing. "You have the time?"

"I'll make it. What's the point of living if you don't enjoy it? Right?"

He had a point there, and that was how she found herself up and on a very tall horse, trotting through hay fields and around the many trails of the Miller farm.

It really was peaceful. Watching the butterflies and dragon-flies all buzzing about, and the ducks and swans in the water. Workers waved to them as they passed, and they stopped for a good half hour to explore and harvest from Ma's garden that was bigger than most people's back yards.

But the real fun part was when they were going around a field where the milk cows were all grazing. Since the Millers were all about humane treatment, they didn't keep their cows continuously pregnant or take their babies away, so it really was something else to see all the growing calves running around and acting like young ones should be able to act—unrestricted and carefree.

If Keiko didn't know better, she would think that cows were just very large, vegetarian dogs.

"Hey, I want you to meet my favorite," Missy said, stopping her horse and swinging herself down. The whole movement was impressive to Keiko considering that the blond's horse was even bigger and taller than her. Then again, Missy was some-where around six-foot tall, so it made sense that she needed a mount that reached her.

Keiko followed suit, and they walked between the grazing cows, Missy clearly on the lookout for something in particular. Keiko reached out every so often, stroking at different cows as she went along. She was always surprised by how warm and soft they were. It almost made her want to cuddle up with one on a starry night, which wasn't like her. She wasn't the most... touchy of people. She liked her personal space.

"Francesca!" Missy let out a sharp whistle and there was a loud bleat in response—or whatever sound it was that young cows made—and suddenly a happy creature came bounding over to them.

Oh, wow, she *was* adorable. Dappled with roan and white, the calf that ran up to Missy had the most ridiculously long lashes that Keiko had ever seen, complete with dainty hooves and what almost looked like freckles below her chocolate eyes.

"Hey there, my little girl. This is my friend Keiko! I don't think you two have met, have you?"

"No, we haven't," Keiko said, crouching down in front of the animal only to receive a lick up the side of her entire face.

Aw, that was sweet... but also really *gross.*

Keiko felt a familiar twist in her stomach, and the urge to scrub her face was almost overwhelming. Quickly she stood, hands scrambling for the sanitizer that she always kept in her pocket.

"Whoops, sorry about that." Missy laughed.

But Keiko's mind was already taking off. She could *feel* germs burrowing into her skin—and she needed to *scrub.* She needed to be *clean.*

She got the sanitizer onto her hands and slapped it right on her face, rubbing vigorously. She could feel her adrenaline spiking, and she had to remember her breathing.

In through her nose, out through her mouth.

In through her nose, out through her mouth.

Calm. Calm.

Germs didn't move in real-time like that. She was fine. She was okay. Discomfort was not lethal.

"Uh, Keiko, are you okay?"

She felt like she had a white-knuckle grip on her own

consciousness, and it took all of her energy to remain calm as she answered.

"I didn't realize how much time had passed. I have a prayer session I need to get to church for."

"Oh, yeah, let's get you back."

"Sophia and I are going to keep riding, if you don't mind," Bradley said. "Missy, can you take her back?"

"Sure, that's no problem. See you around dinner!"

And that was that. No one asked any questions which was a relief. While Keiko had been relatively open about her mental illness with them, she supposed none of them really understood what it was like to struggle with OCD. So many people used the term flippantly, but they didn't understand the rituals, the impossible-to-ignore urges. At the moment, her entire insides were crawling, demanding that she wash her hands. That she touch a knob one time. Two times. Three times. Turn it off. Turn it on.

Except there was no knob in front of her. There was no bathroom. She was on a horse and having to hold still as she rode back towards the Miller house.

It seemed to take an eternity to get there, and when she did, she about ran from the barn to her car, grabbing her wipes from her glove compartment and practically scrubbing the skin of her face off.

She needed to be clean. She had to be clean.

She needed to *breathe*. To calm down.

In through her nose. Out through her mouth. In through her nose. Hold it in her belly. Out through her mouth. She was fine. Discomfort was not lethal. It was okay to be upset. It was okay to be grossed out and to have her skin crawl. None of those things would kill her.

But she needed to get to the church. She was losing control

like she hadn't in a very long time, and nothing quite centered her like the quiet in the church sanctuary. The presence she felt. Like there was something *more*. That there was a purpose for everything, and she wasn't alone.

She went much faster than she should have, but thankfully the few cops in their town seemed to be occupied, because she made it to the parking lot without being stopped. She practically sprinted out of her car and went straight for the women's bathroom.

She burst through the door but skidded to a stop to close it all the way. Before she could think about it, her hand tapped on the handle three times and she flicked the light.

No. That was bad. She wasn't supposed to give in to the rituals. It was a slippery slope and once she started sliding, it was oh so difficult to stop.

Cutting herself off, she rushed to the sink and turned the water on full blast. She allowed herself a moment to be proud that she didn't fiddle with the faucets beyond that, and stuck her hands in.

She spent a good five minutes there, just washing and washing and washing until both her hands and face started to hurt. Breathing deeply, she stood and reached for the paper towels that weren't exactly soft.

She was in the middle of drying herself off when the door opened again, and she recognized the pastor's wife coming in.

"Oh, Keiko, my dear! I didn't expect to see you. You normally take today off. Are you joining us for our prayer circle?"

Prayer circle? Now that sounded like something she could use. Keiko nodded, and the pastor's wife smiled warmly at her. "Well, what a treat. I do have to say, I don't know what we'd do without you. You make such a difference here. I don't think I've ever met a young one who was so obviously in touch with the Lord."

"You really think that?" Keiko murmured, feeling far shakier than she had in a long time. If she was really one with the Lord, why was her mind still flashing to Bryant standing in her living room with no shirt? Why did she wonder what it would be like to taste the sinful apple he was extending to her? Those feelings didn't seem like something a woman who was secure in her faith was supposed to feel.

"Of course, dear. I wouldn't say it if I didn't. We're in the fellowship room, why don't you run along and I'll catch up?"

Keiko nodded and guided herself out. Surprisingly, the woman's words seemed to have worked as a sort of salve, bolstering her so she felt less like she was teetering on the edge. She was able to find the room and settled into a chair, calmly greeting the other women present.

It didn't take long for Mrs. Faltstaff to join them, and soon all of their heads were bowed. It was Mrs. Csapo who said the opening prayer, that took quite a few minutes, but then it was time for everyone to silently go through their own conversations with God.

Keiko was well aware that to outside people, it probably looked silly, but she didn't care. She reached down inside of her, tugging on that connection that burned so brightly in the still and peace of the church.

She asked for strength. She asked for guidance. She prayed for his grace that she wasn't doing wrong and overstepping her bounds. She prayed for wisdom.

And most of all she prayed for Bryant.

Because no matter what ended up happening, the fact of the matter was that he was in pain and unhappy. If there was anyone who could fix that, it was the big man himself.

By the time the whole thing wrapped up, she was feeling much better. Solid and secure and ready to face so many of the challenges that came with life. She said her goodbyes and readied to head back to her apartment, when her forgotten phone rang in her pocket.

It was a short buzz, singular and strong, which meant it was a text. Good. That was something she could ignore. But then it buzzed again. And then again.

While Keiko wasn't attached to her phone like some were, she couldn't ignore that, so she reached in and pulled it out. When she saw Bryant's name across the top, she felt her good mood falter.

Can we talk?

9

Bryant

*I*f someone had asked Bryant a week ago if he would ever allow himself to be stuck on a single woman, he would have laughed right in their face. But that was exactly what had happened to him. In the days after his hasty retreat from Keiko's house, he had found himself thinking about her nonstop.

He guessed that maybe it was because he wasn't used to people resisting his charms. Well, ignoring his charisma like it didn't exist, without acting like they outright hated him. Somehow, Keiko treated him with respect as a fellow adult while also telling him that she didn't entirely agree with how he conducted himself, which was such an alien experience that his mind wouldn't let him shake it.

To be completely honest, he hadn't expected her to answer his texts. And if she hadn't, he would have let it be. He wasn't going to be one of those creepy guys who didn't get the hint and harassed a woman for not bowing to his whims. But to his great astonishment, she did indeed answer, and that was how he ended up waiting for her in the middle of a Bistro in the city.

And the reason he was waiting for her was because she had turned down his offer of picking her up and insisted that she drive herself. He guessed that it took a certain amount of trust to get into a car with a strange man, and he had lost what trust he had before with his stunt in her apartment.

He had just taken off his shirt, something he did every time he went to the beach. But he definitely found himself wishing that he had thought that part through more thoroughly.

He supposed that Keiko could change her mind and not show up, but that didn't seem like her. If she didn't want to come, she wouldn't have agreed to it.

Or at least he hoped so, but as the minutes ticked by, he began to worry more and more.

Ugh. Since when did he worry about being stood up? His entire world had been flipped upside down, and he resented it. He had worked hard to make his life exactly how he wanted it. It wasn't right for her to just swing right in and break all his rules.

"You look like you're thinking entirely too hard."

He looked up from the table, surprised to see Keiko there, smiling politely at him. "That's not something I'm often accused of."

"Huh, I wonder why."

To his great relief, she set her purse down and sat, picking up a menu to look it over. "I've heard your brothers talk about this place, but I've never actually had a chance to come here."

"Well, I'm glad to be the one to treat you then."

"Oh, you're treating me? So I should order the most expensive thing on the menu then?"

"If that's what you want," he said, sagging internally as the tension drained from him. If Keiko was bantering with him, that had to mean that he hadn't completely exiled himself from her grace. "I figure that's a good first step towards an apology."

"Oh?" she murmured, keeping her voice remarkably still. "You need to apologize?"

"Yeah, I would have thought that part was obvious."

"It is, but that doesn't mean I expected it."

"Well, allow me to raise your expectations."

Bryant found it so bizarre how whenever he tried to be smooth with Keiko, it always blew up in his face. But when he just talked to her like a normal conversation, it flowed with an ease that was almost second nature. To him, he felt like the air was crackling all around him with attraction and curiosity, but Keiko always seemed cool as a cucumber with only ever a polite amount of interest in the conversation.

It didn't make sense, none of it made sense, especially not the way he swallowed hard when she affixed him with a soft, genuine grin.

"In that case, I am glad you reached out. It takes maturity to be proactive about an apology."

Huh. There was another compliment. She was being strangely nice to him considering he'd made her freak so much she'd kicked him out of her house. Her reaction was entirely different from what he was expecting. Whenever he ticked off his family, a solid three months would pass where no one would let it go, bringing it up over and over again any chance they got.

"Do you have any recommendations?"

"Well, I'm a fan of their smoky brisket. The barbeque sauce

on it is delicious, and there's about four different sorts of cheese."

She wrinkled her nose. "I don't like things that will make my hands messy."

"Oh, all right. So, knife and fork, fair enough." Bryant quickly ran through everything he usually ate there, and he never realized how much he often ate with his hands. "Um... I think... their pumpkin ravioli is pretty good."

She nodded but continued to study the menu.

It felt surprisingly natural to sit there quietly, just in each other's presence as they decided what they wanted to eat. When the server came to take their order, it almost startled Bryant, he had been so at peace and calm. That was unusual for him. It always felt like his head was spinning off in some direction, thinking about either work, or his next expansion, or where he was going to get his next thrill.

Strange.

In the end, he ordered what was basically a fancy version of an appetizer sampler and the rib platter for himself, while Keiko went with a chicken breast dish. It was the first boring thing she had done.

He also noticed that she didn't order any alcohol. He got himself a single stout, but she just got water.

Not soda.

Water.

Interesting.

And by interesting, he meant not at all.

He'd taken plenty of women out to a lot of amazing places, and there was a certain trend he was familiar with that Keiko was beginning to present.

Some women, mostly because of society's stupid obsession with thinness, didn't like to eat anything substantial in front of a man they were trying to impress. It was something he found kind of annoying, and he was beginning to think that maybe Keiko was doing all that.

The good thing was that meant that she was actively trying to impress him. The bad thing was that it was annoying, trite, and predictable. Maybe he'd overestimated her?

Or maybe he was just overthinking everything. Maybe he was trying to find a fault in her so she felt more on his level.

"I can see you thinking again," she said, tilting her head and looking him over.

Bryant had been given the elevator eyes plenty of times in his life, but it usually carried a much different connotation. With Keiko, it felt like she was looking *inside* of him, into all the little cracks and cervices he had inside that were hidden by his carefully curated and polished veneer.

"I get the feeling that you can see what most people are thinking."

She did let out a slight chuckle at that, which eased some of the tension lancing up and down his spine.

"I do have a knack for reading people."

"So, you're just that empathetic?"

She gave the politest version of a shrug he had ever seen, always poised. "Perhaps. I don't know if that is it. To me, it feels more like being able to put together different pieces of a puzzle."

"What do you mean?"

She opened her mouth to answer but was interrupted as their appetizer came out. He noticed that she instantly went for her silverware even though almost all of it was finger food, and she actually used one of the mini-plates that came with it to carefully place a single piece of the artisanal bread and a small bit of cheese right on top of it, before cutting it in two.

He watched, mystified, as she speared the one half with a fork, brought it to her mouth, and chewed for a good minute before swallowing.

Who ate what was essentially the rich man's version of cheese and crackers with a knife and fork?

"So let's say I notice that I'm talking to someone, and their facial expression falls when I mention a certain thing. The most obvious answer is that they don't like those things, but perhaps there's more to it. The why they don't like it, or the how. It's almost like... an investigation of sorts, where I pick up all these little clues until I can put together a clear picture."

"So, what, you're like Sherlock Holmes?"

"Hardly," she said with a wan smile, "but deductive reasoning is actually the least accurate form of riddle solving and actually the most prone to errors, if you were ever curious."

"Is that so?"

"That is why I said it."

"All right then," Bryant sat back, arms open. "What kind of case are you putting together against me?"

Her gentle smile faltered. "I don't think that's a good idea."

He leaned forward conspiratorially. "Why? Because you're afraid to admit you find me charming? Interesting? Handsome, even?"

"Your attractiveness is relatively objective, so I don't see why I would need to admit that. But no, it's because people don't actually like having what they think are their inner secrets just plucked out of them."

"That's because most people don't realize how obvious they are."

"It's because most people build walls for a reason and having some girl who works part-time at a library get inside of them is alarming."

"Aw, come on," Bryant coaxed. "I'm a big boy, I can handle it."

She set her fork down, looking him over with that soul-searching gaze once more. "It's difficult to even know where to start."

"Is it? Because I'm just that complicated?"

"No, you're just that hurt."

Hurt?

"For example, your whole situation with your family. You would like most people to think that you don't care, that you're all wrapped up in the limelight and the partying, but that's not true.

"Their rejection of you hurts you, deeply, and your response is to do more things to punish them. If they're going to cast you out of their lives for questioning things, for being what you perceive to be yourself, then you're going to be the worst of everything they see you as."

She continued on, her tone matter-of-fact and unjudgmental. She could have been reading a grocery list for all the emotion she put into it. "The issue is you're smart. Too smart. You enjoyed the challenge of getting to where you are, but now that you're basically guaranteed success with all your accrued wealth, you're bored. Life is empty for you without something to puzzle over, something to solve.

"Sure, the women, wine, and wealth are nice. They serve as pleasant distractions. But they're like cotton candy, aren't they? All spun sugar and sweetness but no satiation. You're craving something, anything to give you true sustenance, and that's why you're so interested in me.

"I'm a challenge to you. I disapprove of your wealth and your ways. I'm a part of a world you hate. But I respect you, and I talk to you as an equal. I don't think you're lesser for your choices, and I don't think it's my place to judge you. You don't know how to unite those two ideas because you've so neatly separated the world into predictable patterns."

Bryant stared at her, feeling flayed out and open in a way he hadn't in a long while.

None of that was true! He *loved* his life! Better than living on some backwater ranch his whole life and standing in the shadow of all his brothers.

And yet... her words still stung. Like someone had poured salt right down his gullet and was making it sit in his stomach, combining with the acid there until pure vitriol was bubbling through him.

"You're upset," she said, pursing her lips together. "I told you; people don't like being psychoanalyzed." She lifted her fork again and took another bite of the other half of her cheese and bread. She looked only mildly concerned, her expressions trained into that same banal mask.

"Am I?" Before he could think it through, that burning, blackened anger was sliding acrimoniously over his tongue.

"I did not say those things to hurt you, and you *did* ask. I was only saying things that I've observed. They were not judgments on your character."

"Really? Because it certainly felt that way. I know you like to hold onto this constant poise, this unperturbable attitude, but I think you're full of crap."

"Bryant—"

"Because I can do the same thing to you. That false aplomb is just a charade. In reality, you're just some little girl who's just smart enough to realize how big and wide the world is, and that makes you feel out of control. You see, control is something you crave, desperately so, and pretending that you have an insight into everyone's mind is how you play into your own fantasy.

"You think you're above all of us, with our problems and our emotions, but the reality is that they rule you more than anyone else. Everything about you is carefully constructed, from that pious churchgoer schtick to even how you look."

"How I look?"

A small voice inside of him begged him to stop. He knew he was losing his temper and saying things just to hurt, but his mouth just kept right on going.

"You want people to think that you're some natural slender and beautiful girl, blessed by God or some crap like that, but look at what you've done at this meal. You could have anything you want, but you chose plain water. And you just ate a single hors d'oeuvre with a knife and a fork.

"You could have anything from the menu, anything you wanted, but you chose a single chicken breast and steamed vegetables. I'm sure if they had salad entrees around here, you would have just gotten that.

"Because the reality is, you're boring, and you're powerless, and your entire world is shaped by everyone around you. You like to think that you're some insightful rebel, but really your biggest concern is calorie counts and what other people think of you."

Finally, he ran out of both air and hate, leaving him feeling vaguely deflated. It wasn't the best position to receive Keiko's no-doubt scathing rejoinder, but instead of biting his head off like she was supposed to, she simply stood.

"I apologize, but I think I've lost my appetite. Enjoy your meal, Bryant."

But wait, that wasn't how it was supposed to go! Hadn't she ever been in a fight before? She was supposed to yell at him, then he would yell at her, followed by her screaming and then they'd figure it out. Finally, he'd buy her something to make up for it.

"Keiko—"

"No," she said firmly, pushing her chair in with shaking hands. "I am quite done with this conversation. Sophia was right. It was arrogant of me to think that I am qualified to fix anyone, least of all you."

She tipped her head, and he saw the tiniest of cracks in her impassive veneer. But instead of seeing anger behind those little fissures, or defiance, he only saw a raw sort of hurt that made guilt instantly fill where his anger had just been.

And then she was gone, heading out the door. Bryant was flooded with so many emotions that he could only sit there and watch where she exited, everything turned on its head again.

He was gobsmacked. He was embarrassed. He was confused at what had just happened. Hurriedly, he threw a hundred on the table and left, going to his own car. He felt as if he was in shock, actually. He had been so prepared for a fight and all the release of adrenaline that would come with that. But instead, it was just... nothing.

His mind was spinning its wheels for so long it wasn't until he buckled his seatbelt when her last words hit him.

...fix him?

10

Bryant

*K*eiko's words wouldn't leave his head.

He was being haunted by what she'd said, the phrase repeating itself over and over again until it was practically a continuous loop. It followed him into his dreams; he found himself absently typing it into emails. Even his business meetings could barely fit into his brain over the constant puzzling.

He didn't need fixing. Fixing implied that he was broken, which he most certainly wasn't. And it didn't make sense considering how much she'd complimented him. Unlike his family, she seemed to appreciate his head for business. She'd even called him smart. That was part of what made him think he was winning her over.

But no, apparently the entire time she'd been trying to "*fix*" him.

He felt tricked, like she had only spent time with him because of some ulterior motive. But hadn't he been doing the same to her? Sure, she seemed to have been well aware that he was only interested because she defied his expectations, but that wasn't much different.

He found no peace, even over the weekend where he got well and truly blasted at a movie premiere party in Cali, and the more days that passed, the more disquieted he grew, until it felt like his entire skin was prickling.

He needed to talk to somebody, but who? Most of his friends were from his business or the party scene, and he didn't exactly want to go and let them know about the most vulnerable parts of himself or that he was borderline obsessed over a chick from his hometown.

So, he found himself driving all the way from the city to the Ranch on a Tuesday, hoping he could talk to Bradley.

As far as he knew from the wedding, Benji's new bride was Keiko's best friend, so Benji *probably* was the best person to talk to, but they were still on their ridiculously long honeymoon.

Not that Benji would have helped him anyway. His eldest three brothers were very much not huge fans of his— although at least the middle brother wasn't nearly as snappish as Ben, who seemed to take Bryant's lifestyle as a personal affront.

When he arrived, he realized that he didn't want to go into the house where he would see Ma or Pa or anybody else. He was so tired, so strung up, he just couldn't handle any of their disapproving looks.

Or that particular look of hurt that would always settle on Ma's face. They were the ones who made him how he was; what gave them the right to look at him like *that?*

He texted Bradley, half expecting his brother not to answer

him. Between being caught up in his work and wanting to avoid drama, connecting with his closest brother in age was difficult.

But really, he was the only one Bryant had any sort of bond with at all. He understood what it was like to not fit in. They both had been into unusual things when they were young. While Bradley had been books and theater, Bryant had been all about comics. And games. And movies. He had been much more content sitting inside and going about his various activities than going outside and wrestling around like all of his brothers.

And that was where it had started. He hadn't realized it then, but it was the first instance of the family realizing maybe he wasn't quite like them. And instead of just enjoying that difference, they kept trying to "encourage" him to be more like them, to not like such weird things. And the more they pushed, the more he resisted until finally, resentment had already taken hold.

Funny, it probably had seemed like such a small thing at the time, but it had certainly grown its roots and was no tiny issue now.

He was so absorbed in his thoughts that he jumped when there was a soft knock on his window. Surprisingly, it was Bradley, looking concerned.

"Hey, surprised to see you so soon."

"Yeah," Bryant said flatly, getting out of his car and looking around. "Can we go for a walk?"

Bryant almost expected him to say no. If Bradley was in the middle of a project or a spreadsheet, not even God himself could steer the man away. That was why he was so surprised when he heard his elder brother had gotten himself a fiancé.

"Uh, sure. I s'pose I got the time."

Bryant sagged in relief and headed out. He remembered an

older path that he used to love when he was younger, mostly because it was lined with blackberry vines and blueberry bushes and mulberry trees so he could munch whenever he wanted to.

"So, what's going on? I've been seeing you around more lately. Normally you try to avoid the family as much as possible."

"Yeah, I, uh... have had a project in town."

"Ah, and by a project, do you mean you've been infatuated with Miss Keiko."

Bryant grimaced at that. "How do you know?"

He shrugged. "Sophia confides in me often."

Sophia? Right, the name of his girl. But that was also who Keiko had mentioned, which meant that she knew about the plan to "fix" him from the start.

"Gotcha. Yeah, well it's not going well, so you won't be seeing me too often."

"That's probably for the better," Bradley said with a sigh. "You should leave Keiko alone. She's a good person, you know?"

Something about his words spiked down into Bryant and he felt his hackles rise. "What do you mean by that?"

"Nothing. I just... she's sweet, and she's smart. You know, a good person. Sophia likes her."

"So what then, I don't deserve a good person?" He didn't know why he was taking such offense, but he was. All of his brothers had someone. A beautiful woman to confide in, to trust and find respite in. All of their partners were good people; why couldn't he have the same?

"That's not what I'm saying, Bryant."

"Then what are you saying?"

Bradley rubbed his temples as they walked along the trail, the gentle chirping of birds doing nothing to counteract the tension between them. Bryant did feel a flash of guilt. His brother had never been the best with words or emotions, and he was kind of forcing his hand.

"It's just... people like her are few and far between, and she should be cherished for what she is. I get why you would be drawn to her, but she wouldn't be happy or fit into your life, so unless you're willing to change for her, it's only gonna end up hurting her and probably you.

"And don't get me wrong, brother, I love you, but I don't get the impression that you want to change at all. Lord knows Ma has been trying to get you to for years."

"Yeah, they've been trying to change me my entire life," Bryant muttered. "I was never going to be like Ben or Bart, and they've never forgiven me for that."

"Hey, I'm not sure that's true."

"Isn't it? Tell me, Bradley, how often did they take potshots at you until you started doing finances for them and they realized they could make money off you."

"Come on, it's not like that."

"Isn't it? Did Pa ever come to one of your plays?"

"Well... no."

"And in Ma's Christmas letters, did she ever brag about when you got the lead in the spring musical as a sophomore?"

"No."

"But every record of Ben and Bart was in there, right? Or how she dedicated a whole page to when you decided to join the swim team that one year. I'm not saying our parents are cruel or did it purposefully, but they made it abundantly clear what things they valued, what they didn't, and you and I were always the *weird* ones."

"To be fair, almost everyone still thinks I'm weird. They've just learned that it's a good thing."

"Like I said, because you chose to stay here and help them build up the empire. You compromised. You should have gone off to college like you wanted to and explored the world beyond what our parents want."

"...compromise isn't so bad, Bryant. It's not losing. And I benefitted from choosing the path I did."

"Compromise *is* a loss, just one you negotiate."

"Bryant..." Bradley sighed.

Bryant was getting sick of that sound.

Bradley continued, "You know, I get why you're mad, but that's exactly the reason why things keep getting worse and worse. Would it be so bad to just lower your guard a little and maybe *try* to make things work out."

Yes, it absolutely would.

Bradley didn't get it, because he was part of the clan too. He'd forgotten all the awkwardness of being the strange kid in their younger years and was one of the good ones now.

...the good ones.

"Do you think I'm a bad person?" Bryant asked finally, the words coming out inelegantly and plain, but they were what he needed to know.

"I... I don't know how to answer that, Bryant."

Those words stabbed through him, going deeper than even Keiko's barbs. His own brother couldn't answer, because he didn't want to say it to Bryant's face.

He had always seen himself as a playful scamp, a charming ne'er do well who was the anti-hero to his family's pious and old-fashioned judgment. They had all condemned him because they hadn't understood him, not because he was inherently *not good.*

Was his perception that skewed? It didn't seem possible, and yet that was the boat that he was in.

"Hey!"

Both men jumped and were surprised to see Missy riding up to them on Bart's four-wheeler. The tall woman jumped off and strode towards them, her shoulders squared.

Bryant assumed that she was there for some sort of important ranch business, so he stepped to the side. He needed a moment to think anyway. He felt like he was asking himself a bunch of questions he had never even thought he needed to ask and wondering things he had never wondered before.

But all of that came to a screeching halt as Missy stormed right up to him and slapped him straight across the face.

The woman's biceps weren't just for show, and Bryant's head whipped to the side from the force of it. It hurt, but mostly it shocked him, and he looked at the blond incredulously.

"How dare you!" she spat, finger in Bryant's stinging face.

While Bryant had never struck a woman in his entire life, he wondered if he was about to need to defend himself from a very angry in-law.

Missy was right in his face. "Look, it's one thing if you want to ruin your own life, but you have *no right* to treat Keiko like—"

Her words were drowned out by the sound of another four-wheeler, and suddenly Bart was there too. His giant, muscled brother moved impossibly fast, getting between him and Missy and forcing her backward.

"Hey, calm down, honey. Remember what you taught me? We solve things with our words, not violence. You know it's not right to put your hands-on people in anger."

Missy let out a series of swear words that was impressive to even Bryant. He'd never seen the blond bombshell be anything other than happy and laughing, so it was like he was seeing a completely different side of her.

A mean side. A violent side. A side that *he* brought out.

"Come on, honey. Let's go home. That baby rabbit is probably hungry. You can show me how to bottle feed her again."

Missy looked like she wanted to say more, and Bryant was reminded of how a mother coyote would look when defending her pups. The reason why Missy was so riled up was because she thought that he was a danger. A threat.

Was she even wrong?

He didn't know. His first instinct was to dismiss her as crazy. As another Bible-thumping, brainwashed bumpkin that had already decided who and what he was before she ever met him.

But then he thought of how Keiko looked at him when she had left their meal, how his every interaction with her was one that was supposed to get him something, like she was nothing more than a prize to be won, a thing to be used. He thought of the slight tremor in her hand and the pain written across her features.

But his thoughts were cut off as Bart turned to look back over his shoulder, face in a snarl.

"Stay away from her friend. You've done enough damage as it is."

His tone. That same condescending, reproachful tone that he'd heard since he was a kid, burst through the lines that he had been connecting and all of a sudden, all he could feel was anger. He didn't deserve this; he didn't deserve any of this. He'd come around to talk out some things that he needed to figure out with his one brother who would listen to him, not be attacked.

The four-wheelers raced off, and Bryant stormed back towards his car. Bradley didn't even try to stop him, just standing somewhere on that stupid trail, no doubt wondering what the hell had just happened.

It took him longer than he would have liked to finally reach the lot that the workers used, but once he was there, he practically vaulted into his souped-up ride and peeled out of there. He didn't care if he kicked up dust and dirt. He just needed to *go*.

Was he a bad person?

No. He just liked to have fun. They were all jealous because they were ruled by all these little rules from a stupid old book. Rules that they broke whenever *they* wanted to, judging by the stinging red mark on Bryant's face.

Whatever. He didn't need them. He didn't need Keiko. He had everything he needed, and he was perfectly content with his life.

In fact, he was going to go enjoy himself a good time, something his family probably all wanted but would never allow themselves. Because, unlike them, he was *free*.

11

Keiko

*H*er fingers ached as she cleaned the mirror in her bathroom for the fifth time. But it seemed no matter how many times she squeegeed it, there was always a thin line of film somewhere.

She had to get it off. Film was dirty, and dirt was germy, and germs made her skin crawl to the point where she wanted to tear it off. She had to get rid of them, she had to—

The handle of her cleaning tool broke, snapping her out of the spiral. She took a deep breath. She knew that she was stuck in a cleaning bender but couldn't quite seem to get out.

She'd gone over her apartment twice, and the only thing that had managed to slow her down was that she'd had to take all of her laundry to the laundromat down the street. But then she'd just ended up sweeping and mopping and wiping down the machines there, so that wasn't exactly any sort of break.

She was tired, and she just wanted to sit around and enjoy herself considering how stressful her life had recently become, but she couldn't. She felt like she was teetering on the edge of the cliff and the only thing that was going to keep her from falling over the edge was to make sure that every single molecule of her apartment was spick and span.

It was exhausting, but there was no reprieve. All of her coping mechanisms were coming up empty and her support was AWOL.

Well, perhaps that wasn't exactly accurate. It was just that Dani was still on her honeymoon. Keiko missed her terribly. Dani was always there to wind her down, or remind her to relax, or cook delicious food that she couldn't resist. Dani also had just enough problems that Keiko would occasionally need to help her too, and aiding someone always made Keiko feel better.

But it wasn't like her whole world revolved around her best friend. She'd called her therapist as well to see if her office could schedule an emergency appointment. But unfortunately, the doctor was out with the flu and Keiko didn't gel very well with the other therapist who worked in her office. And as if that wasn't enough, they warned her that they might have to cancel Keiko's Friday appointment as well.

So she was mostly on her own. She supposed she could call her parents, but she knew what they would say. They would ask if she wanted to move back home. They would give her an out that would be so easy to take, but she knew she couldn't. Part of her therapy was pushing herself to get out of the protective bubble she had built and learn to live on her own. And while her parents did always try their best, they were sometimes too enabling.

Her pause allowed her mind to remember that she actually

had a body to take care of, and it took a quick inventory of what was going on. Her hands ached from scrubbing, her fingertips were all dry and cracked from the harsh cleaning agents, her back hurt, and she was hungry.

She was really, *really* hungry.

When was the last time she had even eaten? Was it the day before? She had thought she had eaten breakfast, but now that she thought about it again, she'd been distracted by the need to sterilize her sink, then her counters, then wash all of her dishes.

Geez, she was not in a good way. The only thing that wasn't really going wrong was that she wasn't giving in to her rituals, even though it was sorely tempting.

Ugh. She shouldn't have thought about that, because suddenly she felt like she needed to check the lock on the door. Had she locked it? She didn't remember locking it.

She should lock it.

She took a hurried step toward it before clamping down hard on that thought. No. *Food.* She would take care of her needs, and then she could clean and check the door as much as she wanted.

Keiko went to her small kitchen and looked over all the food. Suddenly, she was far too exhausted to cook anything, exhaustion filling her to the brim. If she tried to make something from scratch, she'd never actually make it.

All right, so a full meal was out. Searching some more, she found a box of granola bars and grabbed one.

The bar tasted like chalk in her mouth and went down like ash, but at least it was calories. If she recalled right, they were the ones that had extra protein, but she wasn't willing to dig through the trash for the wrapper.

But she did desperately need to brush her teeth. Rushing to the bathroom, she grabbed her supplies from where she kept them in the medicine cabinet and went about brushing her teeth.

And then brushing her teeth again.

Then again.

No matter how much she scrubbed, she could still feel the crumbs along her gums. It was like little bugs all in her mouth and she wanted to scream.

Where was her medicine? She had medicine for times like these. She should probably take it.

But instead she kept on attacking her teeth. It was on her fifth round of brushing and gargling mouthwash, frustration so high that she felt like she could burst into tears at any moment, that a knock sounded on her door.

Hearing the knock was like someone flipped a switch in her. She was able to set her toothbrush down and finally rinse her mouth. Crossing to the door, she resisted peeking out of the eyehole and unlocking then locking the door three times. Instead, she opened it up.

Huh. She hadn't expected for Bradley Miller to be there.

"Hey there," he said sheepishly. "Can I come in?"

"Of course," she answered, opening the door and forcing a friendly smile onto her face.

This was good. She had a guest, which meant she didn't have to concentrate on herself and instead, could think about being a good host.

"Here, have a seat," she said, stepping to the side. "I'll put some tea on."

"Thanks, Keiko, that's awful nice of you."

She nodded and hurried to her kitchen, going through the motions of brewing some loose-leaf. She chose one of her anxiety blends that was full of chamomile and other soothing things. Lord knew she could use them.

It didn't take long for the water to boil in her electric kettle and a few minutes later, she was bringing two mugs out into her small living room.

"So, to what do I owe the honor of this visit?"

When she thought about it, only Dani and Bryant had ever been in her home. Usually when she hung out with the Millers, she went to their place or to the city.

The man flushed, and Keiko couldn't help but wonder what was going on.

"Uh, see, that's the thing. I'm not quite sure this is the right thing to do, but I'm going off what I've been hearing from Sophia and everything else that's happened and..." he trailed off, looking troubled.

Keiko couldn't help the sinking feeling in her stomach.

"You can say whatever you need to say, Bradley."

"Well, it's just that I was wondering if you would be able to check on my brother, Bryant. Because I've heard from Sophia that you two know each other, and right now... I guess I just feel like my brother needs something. Something my family isn't giving him."

That was about the last thing that she had anticipated, and she sipped at her tea slowly. "And you think I have that thing?"

"I don't know, to be honest. But what I do know is that my brother is in more pain than anybody I know. He's almost as bad as Bart was when he first came home." Bradley shifted, licking his lips like he was trying to find the right words. "I know my brother has a rebellious streak a mile wide and real bad temper, but the thing is, at his heart he's this kind, creative guy who just wants to make things and solve puzzles.

"We didn't have the easiest childhoods, ya know, always being compared to our brothers, but he definitely took it so much worse than me. And I don't blame him, but I think all of that... resentment, I guess, let something dark take root in him and now he's swallowed by it."

Keiko nodded, gleaning more information, feeling her brain shake off all the sticky webs of her spiral. "He didn't fit in as a kid?"

"Lord no. While Ben and Bart were wrestling calves, he wanted to play wizards and dragons dressed up in a curtain. When they were playing sports, he was drawing his own comics and joining a LARPing thing in the city. Even when Benji was doing really well in football and my family had *kinda* accepted my love of school musicals, he was the weird one who joined the Mathletes and mock-trail. He was always the odd one out. While I could kinda grab onto a sliver of likeness and I *liked* my solitude and time away from my brothers, I could tell that he just wanted to be accepted."

Keiko spoke up. "It hurts him, you know. To be rejected by your family. I know you all must mean well, but there's a disconnect in your communication."

"I know. But a few days ago, Bryant actually came to me to ask for my advice. And you know what, I felt like he listened. He's never done that before, and that made me wonder what could have changed. But then some... stuff happened, and I put two and two together, so I figured that maybe you might be able to help him."

Keiko couldn't help it. Part of her pride perked up at the thought that someone she respected thought she could be of use.

"Where is he now?"

"Honestly, I don't know. But I figured you'd be able to figure it out. I remember how you always loved a good mystery."

"I do have a penchant for riddles," she admitted pleasantly. Meanwhile, her head was whirring.

Was she really in a good mental spot to help someone who had partially triggered a near-meltdown? It seemed that her hurt and his hurt could be too volatile together. It would probably be healthiest to call someone better equipped.

"Why not go look for him yourself?"

"You know how it is. A lot of times it's the whole family vs. Bryant, so I don't blame the youngest sibling for feeling ganged up on and not wanting to see any of us right now. He's been ignoring my calls and texts for days.

"As for a professional, I guess it's mostly because I don't really trust most of 'em, and I don't want things leaking to the news. You know how people like to gossip."

She did indeed, especially about the Millers.

"And you trust me?"

"Of course. We've been friends for years. You're one of the good ones, Keiko. You know that Chastity credits you with her and Ben managing to get together. And Dani n' Benji too, for that matter. And right now, I'm pretty sure that Bryant needs a real friend."

"Well, I'm pretty sure we're not friends, but I'll help. You can count on me, Bradley."

"Thanks, Keiko, I really appreciate it. You're such a lifesaver."

She could only hope.

12

Keiko

*K*eiko liked puzzles. She liked finding clues and stringing them together and making a solid picture. What she didn't like was pouring through all of Bryant's different social media pages, trying to find clues to where he could be.

From what she could tell, he was two cities over, hopping around and having a wild time. She found pictures of him winning at a craps table, other shots of him at bars, and drunken tweets about parties he was going to attend.

It was a Thursday, which was a pretty dead day for almost all events, so that was good. She could Google what sort of adult-related entertainment was going on and deduce from there. If she left now and drove, she could get there in about four hours, which would put her there about eleven pm at night.

Not bad.

She rushed to her car, making sure to grab another granola bar and a bottle of water, then she was heading to their one gas station in town.

A thrill went through her. She always did enjoy a challenge, and she definitely was in the middle of one. This was serious, though. She had to remind herself that Bryant could potentially be in a bad situation and that his brother was counting on her to help.

Oh well, at least it was a good distraction for her. She felt more in control. She was needed, she was wanted, and she was doing God's work.

Or at least she hoped she was. Lately, she felt like the connection between her and him was shakier than it normally was.

Then again, the best thing to do when her certainty was waning was to pray, so she did just that as she drove along.

She prayed for a lot of things. She prayed silently, and in song, and in just about every way she knew how. She asked for strength and for mental fortitude. She asked for grace and understanding.

She prayed for Bryant, his family, and she prayed for herself.

The truth was, she was still quite hurt at what he had said to her. So much of it hadn't been true, but the thought that that was how she came across had shaken her to her core.

Yes, she did have a very strict way of holding herself and interacting, but that was how she best managed her mental health. Yes, she had weird rituals with food, but she'd come such a long way since she would only let herself eat a handful of rice in a single day.

All of her strange "quirks" were ways for her to survive. She hadn't asked for the mental illnesses she had, and she refused to let them defeat her either. Just as someone might live with diabetes or fibromyalgia, there were certain things she needed to do to take care of herself that a completely healthy person might never have to think about.

She wished that she had sat there and talked it out with him, explained to him why he was wrong, but the more he spoke, the more exhausted she had been until finally she just felt like an empty bag of bones that was too weak to do anything.

So yeah, they would definitely need to talk about that, but that could come later. She understood that he was hurt, even deeper than she had guessed, and hurt people hurt other people. The reaction was a classic part of the human condition.

And so, she drove. Out of the countryside, the rolling hills that she knew and loved. Out of the city where her library was, where she met with her therapist and worked through whatever she needed to work through.

She drove without stopping, not even to use the restroom, until she finally arrived at the edge of the city that he was supposed to be in. Just in time too, because her tank was on empty and her bladder was on full.

Keiko took care of both issues before pulling into a mall parking lot to do more social media sleuthing. From what she knew of Bryant, he was trying to handle whatever he was feeling by distracting himself until he was over it. And distractions required constant new stimuli, so he probably was going to a new place every night.

Pulling up the map she had made earlier in her home, she went through his pictures and crossed out all of the places that he'd already visited, and then looked at what was left and still open *and* appealed to his hedonistic but bougie side.

Surprisingly, not a whole lot. There were plenty of dives, but she knew Bryant wouldn't tolerate something like that. She could tell from his reaction to her place that he was used to the finer things in life, even if he had tried to contain it.

There was one club left, four bars, a dance hall, and two gentleman's clubs.

Huh. That was far too much for her to investigate in one night. She needed to narrow it down. She could just wait for him to post on social media, but then he might already be moving on to a new place and she would miss him.

She needed to think. If only she had one more clue, one more iota of information that would get her there.

She puzzled it over, trying to think, before an idea came to her.

If she needed another clue, why not just ask for it?

No. That couldn't work. Could it?

She supposed there was only one way to find out.

Exiting out of the internet on her phone, she pulled up her contacts and dialed out. It rang once. Then twice. Then right before the third ring, the call was accepted.

"Keiko?" Bryant asked, slurring the word and utterly drenching it in confusion.

She let out a long breath. "Hey, Bryant. Can we talk?"

"You don't wanna talk ta me. I've been told I'm *bad* for you. I'm supposed to leave you alone."

His words made her heart sink, but she pushed through it, trying to pick up noises in the background. She could hear thumping, sexy music, but that didn't eliminate much.

"Why do you think that, Bryant?"

"Cause everybody tells me so!"

He was definitely drunk off his behind again, and he

already sounded pretty upset. She felt like she didn't have much time before he hung up.

"What about you?"

"What?"

"Do you tell yourself those things? Do you believe that you're bad for me?"

He was quiet a moment, as if he was trying to understand. "You're a good person, Keiko."

Oh, she hadn't quite been expecting that. "Thank you, Bryant."

"But... but I'm not so sure if I am."

A woman's voice cut in before Keiko could answer. "Honey, who ya talking to there? Are they making you upset? Come on, let Rosie cheer you up."

"Is... issa friend. I think. Keiko, are you my friend?"

"I think we could be, Bryant."

A female voice spoke in the background, "Well, honey, I'm your friend right here. Why don't you give me that phone and let me dance for you?"

The line clicked off, and Keiko was left with a mess of unsaid words in her mouth. She sat there a moment, looking at her phone.

Bryant had sounded so *hurt*. She hated it. Her heart squeezed painfully, but she had to tuck those emotions away. She needed to focus on finding Bryant and getting him somewhere that he could recover. She knew better than most that environment made a huge impact on mental health.

All right, he had definitely been talking to a dancer, so that meant a gentleman's club. There were just two of them, so she had a fifty-fifty shot. However, she had a way of maybe improving her chances.

Going back to the internet on her phone, she looked up the number of the closest one and called them right up.

"Klassic Kitty Kat, what'cha need?"

Keiko forced herself to smile brightly and affect a more valley accent. "Oh, hiya! It's my boyfriend's birthday so I wanna take him out as a treat. He loves this dancer named Rosie. Is she on shift right now?"

Keiko wasn't naïve enough to think that there was only one Rosie in the town, so she was hedging her bets on hoping that they wouldn't be working at the same time.

"Rosie? Naw, sorry doll, she hurt her ankle and is out for the week. But we've got other girls I guarantee you're gonna love."

Keiko grimaced at that. "Aww, what a bummer. Well, I'm sure he'll still have lots of fun. Toodles!"

Toodles? Geez, that was bad, even for her.

Oh well. At least now she knew. Looking up the other club, she punched the address into her GPS and peeled out of the parking lot.

She had a friend to save and not a second to waste.

IT WAS HARD NOT to think that God was looking out for her at least a little when not a single cop pulled her over. While she wasn't speeding dangerously, she definitely was going above the limit.

But she couldn't help it. She needed to get to Bryant as soon as possible. There was too much of a chance that he would move on and then who knew if she would be able to find him.

Still, as determined as she was, that didn't mean that she didn't waver when she pulled into the parking lot of what was most unmistakably a gentleman's club.

Ugh.

While there was nothing inherently sinful about nudity, there was something definitely predatory about most establishments involving exotic dancing. Between customers who got away with too much, owners charging astronomical "rent" for dancers, abuse of how long workers were scheduled and other workplace protections, there was approximately zero things she appreciated about places like the one in front of her.

But still, a friend was in trouble, so she was going to do what she had to.

Striding in, she kept her eyes straight ahead. She knew that she didn't look like she fit in at all, but she didn't care. She was on a mission.

Unfortunately, her mission meant she needed to look around.

Keeping her eyes off the stage, she scanned the audience. It was still relatively early for a gentleman's club, so there weren't a ton of people there. That made it easier for her, but she wasn't able to spot Bryant anyway.

Oh dear, had he already left?

Well, if she wanted to find out, she needed to talk to the last person who had seen him.

Heading over to the bar, she waved down the bartender. "Hey, which girl here is Rosie?"

The man regarded her, his eyes narrowed like he was sizing her up, but she didn't relent. "Look, lady, if your husband is cheating on you, that's your business to take care of at home."

Keiko shook her head. "No, nothing like that. My boyfriend's drunk off his butt and he likes to get both lost and mugged when that happens. He usually will visit Rosie if he comes here, so I'm *really* hoping she saw him and knows when he left."

He was still looking at her dubiously, and she had to wonder how many broken marriages ended up in spats in this illustrious place of business.

"Come on, look at me, I'm a twig. I'm not gonna make any trouble."

"If there's one thing I've learned on this job, it's never to underestimate the strength of a pissed off woman."

"Please, man, I'm begging ya."

Thankfully, he relented. "She just went to the bathroom. Should be out in a few minutes. Red hair, real big on top of her head, pink little dress. You can't miss her."

"Thank you so much!" Keiko pulled a twenty from her purse and slapped it on the counter. "Stay safe now!"

Quickly, she hurried over to the bathrooms, trying to stand casually outside of them. She didn't have to wait long before someone who could only be Rosie came out.

"Hey, pardon me—"

"Listen, lady, if your man's here, that's your problem, not mine. I don't interview everybody, bad for business."

"No, no, nobody is cheating. I just, I think my friend was just in here with you, and I was wondering if you saw whether he left or had an idea where he went to?"

Rosie's green eyes narrowed as she seemed to put two and two together. "Oh, it's *you*. The phone lady."

"Yeah, it's me."

"You know, you did a real number on that guy. I've seen him a few times and he didn't seem like the crying type, but after you called, I thought he was gonna break down. Whatever you are, he doesn't need you in his life."

She went to walk off, but Keiko quickly darted in front of her. "Hold on, I don't think you understand. Look, Bryant is dealing with a lot and I—"

"Yeah, yeah, you want to save him. I know your type. All buttoned up and holy, coming in here and telling everyone we're going to hell for just trying to provide for ourselves. He doesn't need somebody like you in his life."

Keiko's heart squeezed again. She could hear the hurt and anger layering Rosie's voice and could only imagine the terrible interactions she's had to form that opinion.

"You're right," she said quickly, which seemed to surprise Rosie long enough to keep her from walking away. "Bryant doesn't need any of that. I just want to get him someplace safe and let him recover until he's back to his normal self."

"Yeah, and I'm Mother Theresa."

Keiko took a deep breath, centering herself. It was clear that if she wanted to get to Bryant, she needed to make up for a whole lot of Christians who hadn't acted in a very Christ-like way.

"Look, Rosie, I understand why you don't trust me. I'm sure people like me have come in here and made all sorts of judgments about you. Told you things that were hateful and shaming and all sorts of bad stuff.

"But they were wrong. I apologize for every single one of them."

Rosie actually did look completely blindsided by that, staring at her in confusion. "You're trying to trick me."

"No, sister, I am not. A lot of people come to the church for bad reasons. They're looking for power, or a way to be better than everyone else. And then they come and pass judgment on people who dare to act how they don't approve.

"It is only God's place to judge. None of us are holy or equipped. Our only job is to present you with the tools you need to come to your *own* decision, and all the love you need to flourish."

"Yeah, then why don't I usually feel loved by your lot protesting outside my place of work?"

"Because a lot of people have lost the message. The second greatest commandment of all is to love our neighbors like ourselves. You are worthy of love and respect, and anyone treating you otherwise is doing wrong. It is not our place to tell anyone that they're going to hell or damnation, and to put a stumbling stone in your path is literally going against the grace of God. You are beautifully and wonderfully made, Rosie. I would love to help you find other employment, but I do not pretend to understand your situation better than you."

"But..." Rosie's lip wobbled.

Keiko wished she could face off against all the Christians who had hurt her so before. That was the opposite of their call, spitting in the face of everything Jesus taught.

"I... I take off my clothes for a living. Aren't you supposed to call me a whore, or a Jezebel? I've heard some pretty creative ones."

"No, no insults here. Have you heard the story of the woman who washed Jesus' feet with her hair?"

"Uh, no, I've never been much of one for the Bible."

"Well, the gospel of Luke never names her, but she was believed to be either an adulterer or a prostitute. You see, in their culture, the washing of someone's feet was a very important and intimate act. One of hospitality and respect. So, when this woman came forward to wash Jesus' feet after his long travels, several men tried to stop her. They told her she wasn't worthy. But then Jesus told them to leave her be and let her wash his feet.

"He accepted her touch as something good. Something pure. He knew that what she did was not a reason to condemn her, but to open his arms wide and let her in. Another time, he saved a woman who was going to be stoned to death for cheating on her husband. Over and over again, he proved that hate and punishment was not the way of God and that anyone can find holiness through him."

"How... how come I've never heard stories like that before?"

"Because few Christians actually read the Bible. You know, if you'd like to talk about this another time, I'd be happy to give you my number and we can chat one-on-one. I just really need to find Bryant right now."

Keiko reached into her purse and pulled out a sticky note, scribbling down her info as fast as she could to hand it to Rosie, who still looked absolutely flabbergasted.

"Really, you're just handing me over your number just like that? You want to hang out with me, a stripper?"

"You're a human and a sister, Rosie. Exotic dancing is just currently your occupation. Your job doesn't define you."

Rosie shook her head and sniffled, breathing in sharply through her nose which Keiko knew from experience did a good job of drying out tears. "No wonder he was going on and on about you. You're something else, phone lady."

"You know, I've heard that before, but it usually isn't a compliment."

She let out the slightest of chuckles at that. "Come on, I put him in a side room because he really was a mess. Follow me."

Her brain flooded with relief, and she quickly trailed after Rosie as she led her toward the back and to the side. She only briefly thought that this might be a trick before she was ushered into a small room with neon lighting and a plasticky looking couch.

"There he is. You should definitely get some water into him. I've never seen him like this."

Keiko followed her pointed figure to see that Bryant was

actually laying across the piece of furniture, a thin blanket over him and a trash can right beside where his head was resting.

"Can you get him out on your own?"

She thought back to the time she'd had to haul him up into her apartment. "I wouldn't say no to a helping hand."

Rosie nodded. "I'll go get a bouncer. Wait here."

Like she would go anywhere else. While she was happy she came to help her friend, and she was glad that she had been able to talk to Rosie and extend an olive branch, as it were, she still wasn't comfortable in spots like this. There was too much lust and predatory behavior for her to ever really let her guard down.

Thankfully, Rosie returned quickly, a large man behind her. "This is my new friend. Can you help her out?"

"Yeah, no problem. Go get Jersey on the door."

"Aye-aye, Cap'n." Rosie looked to Keiko, her eyebrows raised. "You really okay with talking to me later?"

"Of course," Keiko answered quickly. "I meant every word I said, Rosie."

"...thanks. I'll see you around."

And with that she was gone, leaving Keiko with the bouncer.

He didn't say much, just tipped his head to her before throwing Bryant over his shoulder. The youngest Miller let out a groan and grumbled to leave his bed alone, but otherwise didn't try to fight his movement.

"Make sure he drinks plenty of water and lay him down on his side. I've never seen him like this before."

"You recognize him too?" She had had no idea that Bryant liked to visit this particular city often enough to have even the bouncers know his habits.

"Of course. I never met a guy who could have whoever he

wanted but was still so lonely. It's real sad. I gotta say, I'm happy to see he has someone like you. Most nights he only leaves with whatever business or industry folks he brings here and no one else. He needs someone outside of that world."

"Yeah, I'm starting to get that."

"You be safe now, Miss. I appreciate you not making a scene."

She nodded and slid into the driver's seat. It was going to be a long ride home, but she was ready to do it and get him to her apartment so she could take care of him.

The drive was easy enough at first. She stopped back at the same gas station, bought herself a caffeine-heavy soda, topped off her tank and put the pedal to the metal. She turned her radio up, humming along to the tunes just to keep her mind from spinning off into a spiral. It would do her no good to work herself into a tizzy when she would need to conserve her energy for when she got home.

"I'm moving."

Startled, she looked over to see that Bryant was awake and looking blearily out the window.

"How am I moving?"

"Hey, Bryant, it's me, Keiko. I came to get you. Your brother was really worried about you."

"No, he's not," he murmured with a sigh, letting his head roll back.

Keiko allowed herself a moment to drink him in with her peripheral vision. He really was a handsome man. His jaw was sharp and squared with high cheekbones that made his intense eyes stand out. His hair was thick, and slightly curly, making him look on just the right side of perfectly tousled.

But more importantly, all that pain she had only glimpsed at before was written across his features as blazing as the sun.

"He is. He's the one who asked me to come get you. He's your family."

"My family doesn't care 'bout me. I'm a bad person. A blot on their pretty little tapestry. They prolly just wish I'd disappear. Do them all a favor and just"—he made a small popping gesture with one of his hands—"*poof.*"

"That's not true, you know that."

"You dun know *anything*," he answered, leaning against the door. "You weren't *there.*"

"I know enough, Bryant. And I know that they've gone about things in a way that wasn't always best. But I also know that you love them, and they love you. We can work this out."

He made a sound of disagreement and sank down further into his seat.

"You must think m'pathetic."

"No," she answered as honestly as she could. "I just think you're very sick and you need some help. Some support."

He grunted and fell quiet. Risking a glance over to him, Keiko saw that he was solidly asleep.

Well, that was probably for the better. It would give her more time to think, to come up with a plan for what to do and how to get Bryant to talk to his siblings and his siblings to actually *listen*.

They made it to her place without any other incident, and she found herself faced once more with hauling him up the stairs. Surprisingly, it was much easier than the previous time. Keiko guessed maybe because she hadn't just danced through a reception, but she was grateful, nonetheless.

Once she dumped Bryant on her couch, she went about getting him a glass of water, the wastebasket from her bathroom, and a blanket and pillow. It was all very déjà vu, and she couldn't help but wonder if this was a sign from God. That she was supposed to give him a second chance and try to start things over.

It took a minute to get him settled, and this time she actually bothered to take off his shoes and make sure he was propped up on his side. He fought with her a little, but it was like how a sleepy child might fight off actually going under, and she managed it well enough.

When it was all said and done, she did feel a sense of accomplishment. No matter what happened, she'd helped someone in need, and she had fulfilled her promise to Bradley.

Carefully, she knelt by Bryant's face, running her fingers through his thick hair to get it out of his face. For once, he looked peaceful. Not plotting or scheming or hurt. Just himself.

She never noticed how long his lashes were, or how full his lips were. She wondered, just for a moment, what it would have been like if she had given in to his advances on her, but she quickly dismissed it.

Maybe... in another world where Bryant was healthy and interested in her for altruistic reasons, they could have dated. Maybe it wouldn't be so bad to have someone in her life... *romantically.*

But it was too bad that wasn't the situation she was in, so it would be better not to think about that at all.

Bryant murmured something and she leaned in, trying to listen. He tried once, twice, and then without any warning at all, he *puked all over her.*

Keiko reared back, falling onto her butt without ceremony. She sat there a moment, completely in shock, the too warm and chunky liquid all down her front and partially on her chin.

Oh.

No.

Suddenly the world dropped out from under her, and she was swallowed up by everything she had been trying to keep down.

13

Bryant

*B*ryant woke up conscious of three things. He was in pain. He was thirsty. He smelled *terrible*.

He was definitely the kind of guy who liked to lay in bed upon waking and anticipate his day before it happened, but judging by how his back and head were throbbing, it would do him good to sit up.

So he did— and was struck with the strongest sense of déjà vu he had ever had. It was only after several minutes of blinking dopily that he remembered. He had gotten utterly smashed after his visit to the ranch, and someone had come to wherever he was to take care of him.

... judging by the familiar interior surrounding him, that someone was Keiko.

But why?

Hadn't he ruined everything with her? Last he saw her she

was rushing out of a restaurant because he'd lost his temper. He'd apparently hurt her enough that the normally nurturing Amazon that Bart loved so much had hauled off and slapped Bryant across the face for it.

Something must have happened then, but he couldn't remember what for the life of him, and his head hurt so badly he felt like he couldn't begin to puzzle it out.

Looking around again, he saw that Keiko had left a glass of water out which basically glowed gold and had angels singing around it. He grabbed it quickly, chugging it down so that he felt at least a tad more human.

But once that was done and his tongue stopped feeling like a dried-out sock in his mouth, his bladder made its presence known. Struggling to his feet, he shambled to the bathroom.

He took care of his business, then washed his hands and face, taking several moments to splash his face over and over again. Once he was done, he dried himself off with one of the surprisingly soft hand-towels and felt like he might one day be sober again.

It was only after he glanced at himself in the mirror that he noticed a weird sort of sound. Just on the edge of familiar and barely there, the sound pulled his attention

He wandered out of the bathroom, following it to the kitchen. When he turned the corner, he could only blink stupidly in disbelief at the sight that was waiting for him.

There on the floor, doubled over on her hands and knees, was Keiko, scrubbing at the edge of the tile floor under her sink with a toothbrush. The sight was certainly a shock, and it took him a beat to also realize that there were three other blown-out brushes scattered beside her, hinting that she had certainly been there for quite a while.

"Uh, hey there, Keiko. What'cha doing?' His voice sounded

raspy and thin, no doubt to the abuse his throat had taken, but it was audible.

At the sound of his voice, Keiko jumped up onto her feet, smiling broadly at him. "Oh! You're up! You need something to drink. You need food. I'll get you those!"

Before he could say anything else, she was whirling away from him and practically sprinting to the fridge. One thing for certain, she looked *horrendous.*

Her normally pale face was ruddy and covered in a sheen of sweat. There were deep bags under her eyes, which were completely bloodshot. Her normally gently styled hair was heavy with sweat and plastered to both her head and face. Even her lips looked worse for wear, swollen and cracked like she had been chewing on them all night long.

"Hey, are you okay?" he asked cautiously, taking a very tentative step toward her.

"Yeah! Why wouldn't I be? Did you have a good night's sleep? I'm sorry that my couch isn't very comfortable."

"It's fine, just—"

He winced as she opened the fridge door too hard, slamming it into the wall. She grabbed what looked like a carton of orange juice and turned to him, shaking slightly. But something about how she moved put her off-kilter, and the next thing he knew, the carton of juice was slamming into the floor and spilling everywhere.

"Oh geez, let me get that," he said, feeling like something very important was happening but not really understanding what.

"No, no, it's fine. I got it. I *got it!*" Her voice cracked on that last part, and she managed to knock a roll of paper towels over as she went to grab them. Suddenly she was sobbing, loud, raucous and broken.

Bryant stared at her, absolutely gobsmacked, and tried to think of something that would help. "Look, it's okay! I got it, see?"

Grabbing the fallen paper towels, he quickly bent down and wiped the juice up and put the carton back. While he was busy, Keiko had turned to the sink, crying and hiccupping as she washed her hands.

He waited for her to finish, ready to ask her what he could do to help, but as soon as she turned off the tap, she turned it back on again. Then off. Then on. Then she turned only the hot water on, then the cold, then washed her hands all over again.

"I can still feel the dirt. There's so much dirt. It makes my skin crawl."

Bryant had *no* idea what was going on. It was like he had been shoved into a parallel dimension that was like his own, but important details had been changed. But what he did know was that *something* was very much wrong.

"Hey, can I help you? Keiko. I'm right here. Is there anything I can do?"

She didn't answer, just kept right on washing and washing and washing.

Swallowing, Bryant looked around as if there would be some sort of answer there.

"Is there somebody I can call?"

Keiko stiffened at that, standing straight and for just a moment stopping with her frantic scrubbing. "Yeah. Dr. Hyleir in my emergency contact list."

There it was, something she told him he could *do*. Sliding his own phone out of his pocket, he called her and listened for the buzz.

It led him to the bathroom where her phone was on the back of the toilet. How he hadn't noticed it before, he didn't know, but he grabbed it and quickly hit the button to pull up her emergency numbers. Then he tapped on the contact to call Dr. Hyleir.

It rang only once, and then a woman was answering.

"Dr. Hyleir's office, this is Carolina. How may I help you?"

Uh, what did he even say? "Uh, hi, I'm with my friend Keiko, and something's wrong with her. She doesn't seem to really be able to talk to me, but she told me to call this number that was on her emergency contact list."

"All right, thank you for calling us. For her protection, may I ask this Keiko's last name?"

"It's Albryte. Keiko Albryte."

"Thank you for that info. Can you tell me what kind of state Keiko is in?"

"Right now she's furiously scrubbing her hands in the sink. But before that she dropped a bottle of orange juice and freaked out. Crying and everything. I'm a little freaked out myself."

"I understand sir, and we're very grateful you're helping her. We can't disclose certain information because of HIPAA unless you're on her contact list or she's signed a waiver for you. Has she done that with you, sir?"

"Uh, no. We've only sort of just met. Does that mean you can't help her?"

"Not at all, sir, may I have your name?"

"Uh, it's Bryant, Bryant Miller."

"Oh, I see. Do you have a brother, Mr. Miller?"

"Yeah, four of them actually." An idea came to him. "Oh! My brother might be one of her contacts. Bradley Miller?"

"I can't confirm that, but what I can do is give you some questions to ask her and directions to bring her to us. Do you have a way to write this down?"

"Uh, gimme a second." Grabbing his own phone again, he

pulled open a notepad app. "Yeah."

"Thank you for your speed, sir. The most important thing during this entire process is to remain calm. Right now it sounds like Ms. Albryte is in distress, so you being calm and collected will help her more than anything else."

"Okay, I can do that."

"Perfect. This is our address. You can pull right up to the emergency entrance, and we'll guide her into intake."

He hurriedly wrote down everything she said. The clinic was in the city, which was at least an hour's drive away. That thought made him nervous. He knew Keiko wasn't having a heart attack or a stroke, but that didn't make whatever was going on any less scary.

"Now Mr. Miller, I need you to go to Keiko and ask these questions calmly and slowly."

"Okay." He left the bathroom and walked to the kitchen where Keiko had thankfully stopped washing her hands, but was back on her hands and knees, this time scrubbing around the oven.

"Hey, Keiko, when was the last time you slept?"

"Yesterday," she answered shortly, not even bothering to look at him.

"Yesterday as in last night?"

She shook her head. "No. Before work. Then I got you. Then I... cleaned."

"Could you hear that?" he asked the phone.

"Yes, I could Mr. Miller, thank you. Now please ask her when her last meal was."

"Hey, Keiko. Have you eaten lately?"

She shook her head.

"Could you try, for me?"

Another shake of her head.

"Mr. Miller, I know this is difficult, but it would be best if you could get something into her. She has emergency medicine for episodes like these, but they are very hard on an empty stomach."

"So what, I have to make her eat?"

"The best thing to do is to try to coax her. You can try outright force, but Keiko has known food aggression and you could end up injuring the both of you."

"How am I supposed to get her to eat then? I've never done anything like this before!"

"It's all right, Mr. Miller. I can tell you that when Keiko is manic, she does have a people-pleasing streak. The best way to get her to eat might be if you convince her that doing so will help you."

"Uh, okay." He walked carefully around Keiko and went to the fridge. There were a lot of fresh ingredients in there, but he also spotted a lot of easy, simple snacks that were quick and clean to eat. Rooting around, he grabbed what looked like one of those peanut butter and jelly sandwiches with no crust and crossed to sit next to Keiko.

"Too close," she said, sweat dripping down her nose. "You're in my space."

"Oh, sorry." He scooted away and then made a big show of taking a bite of the mini-sandwich and groaning at how good it was. He noticed Keiko's eyes slid over him for just a second before going back to the floor. "That was so good, but my tummy is kind of hurting. You know, it makes me feel *so* bad to waste food, but I don't think I can stomach this. Man, I just feel so *guilty*."

"No, it's okay. I got you. Don't worry. I can take care of you." Her hand flashed out, and abruptly the sandwich was no longer in his hand. Keiko was quickly shoveling it into her mouth.

The sandwich was gone in three bites which she hardly chewed before swallowing and quickly returning to her scrubbing.

"Has she eaten?"

"Yeah, she did."

"Perfect. Now she needs her medication, then you can bring her to us. It should have a red label with a warning for emergencies only. I can disclose to you that, in her notes, she agreed to keep it in the top drawer of her dresser."

"Her dresser? All right."

"Mr. Miller, if it's not there, don't go looking for it and bring her straight here. Sometimes in these situations, a manic person will hide or tamper with their medication. It's not worth the risk if the bottle's not in the agreed-upon spot."

Although he was rushing from task to task without hesitation, Bryant had to admit that he was terrified out of his skull. He'd never been in such a serious situation before, and he felt like his every move was either life or death. Not exactly what he wanted to do when his brain still felt thick and sluggish from all the alcohol he'd had the night before.

He raced toward the only room he hadn't been in and made a beeline for the dresser. Sure enough, there was a bottle there, with its safety seal still on.

"All right, I got it."

"Perfect. Now just get Ms. Albryte to take one and come straight here."

"Shouldn't we do an ambulance or something?"

"We could, but Ms. Albryte has had incredibly adverse reactions to official transport in the past. Considering that she is technically not in a lethal situation, it would be best if people she trusted transported her here."

"All right, if you say so."

Like he was someone she trusted. She had just hauled his hide from a strip club four hours away, and he still had no idea why.

He opened the bottle and pulled a pill out, heading right back to the fridge. Everything swirled in his brain as he got her a glass and filled it with water then crouched next to her again.

"Hey, Keiko, I got this candy and I'm not sure I like it. Will you try it for me?"

"Candy?" she asked. "No. It's sugar. I've had too much already."

He recalled the careful way that she had eaten at their very short dinner and wondered if maybe some sort of eating disorder was connected to whatever was happening in front of him. "That's why I want you to try it. It's sugar and calorie-free so I think it's probably gonna be gross. Won't you try it for me in case it is?"

"Okay." She took it, putting it on her tongue and taking the water.

"Apparently you swallow it whole. How strange is that?"

For some reason, Keiko trusted him and swallowed it down. He heaved a sigh of relief, but she just seemed confused.

"It didn't taste like anything."

"Huh. That's weird. But it was so nice of you to do that for me."

She smiled brilliantly at him, and it actually made his chest ache.

Then she spoke quickly, "Of course. Don't worry, I'm here to take care of you."

"Is that so?"

"Yeah! You'll see. I'm really good at taking care of everyone. I just have to make sure everything is clean. I don't want you getting sick."

Was this how she felt when he was drunk off his butt? Probably not, because it was his own fault that he drank, while it was definitely not her fault for whatever was going on.

"You're so thoughtful, Keiko. I'm grateful to have someone like you looking after me."

She practically glowed at that, and he felt sick about everything that he had put her through. It was obvious the girl was very sick, and yet all she cared about was making sure he was okay.

He had to get her to someone who could help. "Do you think you could come on a car ride with me? I'm too scared to go on my own."

"Yeah, of course. You don't have to worry."

She wasn't looking at him again, busy with cleaning, but it was a step in the right direction.

Standing, he looked around for his keys before remembering that he hadn't driven himself to the city or to Keiko's place. Right. So he needed her keys.

He went on a hunt for them only to find them hanging from a keyring by the door. Of course. But as he gripped them, he realized that while he was pumped full of adrenaline, he definitely wasn't sober enough to drive. And considering everything that was going on, he wasn't going to risk Keiko's life in that way.

He hated bringing anyone else into the situation, especially since he had a sense that it was something incredibly private to Keiko. He could call a cab from the city and just foot the bill, but he hated the thought of how long that would take. Two hours at the quickest and most likely somewhere around three hours.

No. That wouldn't do at all. Whipping his phone out, Bryant dialed Bradley without hesitation.

14

Bryant

*I*t seemed to take forever for Bradley to actually show up, but in reality, it was probably less than fifteen minutes.

To his brother's credit, when Bradley did pull up in Ben's extended cab truck, he didn't ask any questions. He just held the door open for them to pile in, then got in to drive.

What he wasn't expecting was for Dani to already be in there, and she took Keiko into her arms instantly.

"Hey girl, I heard you're not doing too well."

Suddenly Keiko was bursting into tears. "Dani, I feel *terrible*," she whimpered, practically melting into her friend's embrace. "I'm so glad you're back. I drank all these energy drinks so I could stay up and clean, but I'm so tired. I just want to sleep, but I can't because everything is so dirty. It's making me crazy. Am I crazy?"

"No, you're just worn out right now, sweetie. Just like freshman year of college. But you got through that, and you'll get through this too. Why don't you just lean against me and relax, okay? I'm real clean, I promise."

Keiko whimpered again and buried her face in Dani's soft neck. "He threw up on me. I had to get the vomit off, but then I could smell it everywhere."

Dani's gaze flicked to Bryant and there were a whole lot of questions there, but thankfully no hate or anger. Not that he didn't feel that for himself. In fact, he was downright miserable because now he knew what had set Keiko off.

It was very clear she had some sort of issue with things being messy or dirty, and he was pretty sure she'd just said that he'd thrown up either on or near her, which was a pretty terrible way to pay back the woman who was going above and beyond trying to help him.

Her current meltdown was all his fault, really. Keiko seemed healthy and poised when they first met, and now she was a trembling mess. He really did sow destruction wherever he went. Missy was right; he should have stayed away from her.

He really was a bad person.

That thought and other dark ones like it played in his head over and over again on the hour drive to the city. It was pretty tense inside of the cab, and the only one who really talked was Dani.

At least Keiko seemed to settle down a little and fall asleep against her friend, who was humming what Bryant vaguely recognized as a soft lullaby. It was pretty soothing, and if he wasn't full of so much shame and self-hatred, he might have relaxed too.

But, as it were, he was wound as tight as a jack-in-the-box when they finally reached the psychiatry center. Dani helped

Keiko into the intake center. Bradley drove the truck off to the parking garage, taking Bryant with him.

Unsurprisingly, when he finally found a spot, his older brother put the truck into park and just sat there for a moment.

"Should we go in?" Bryant asked, feeling so empty and exhausted he almost wondered if he would float away the moment he stepped outside.

"Are you all right?" his brother asked abruptly. "You've never called me for help, and that seemed like a pretty tense situation."

"I'm not the one that you should be worried about. Keiko's the one who's sick."

"Yeah, but you were there with her. I don't claim to know what happened but doesn't seem like something that's exactly easy to deal with."

"I'm fine. It's fine."

But he wasn't fine. He had no idea what had happened or what Keiko was sick with, but he couldn't help but think that it was absolutely his fault.

"You know that you don't have to deal with things on your own. You've got family."

He couldn't even bring himself to snort at the idea. "Yeah, because we all know how much comfort I draw from them."

"Hey." His brother reached over, his rough and calloused hand resting on Bryant's arm. "You did the right thing by calling me. I'm here for you. And if you'd let them, everyone else would be too."

Bryant closed his eyes and pictured that. Going home and having Ma push a glass of cool lemonade or iced tea into his hand; Pa reading a book in the living room but his eyes would glance up for a moment of recognition and assurance. Bart could clap him on the back and tell him that they should go fishing. Ben would nod and ask him how he was.

It was a pretty picture. A tempting one. It made his heart ache and a bitter sense of longing bloomed within him.

But it was just that, a fantasy. His ties with his family had been severed for so long that there was no hope of repairing them. Besides, why would he ever want to fight and claw for an ounce of recognition and acceptance when the family had long since taught him that he would never be good enough?

Bryant chewed his lip, looking out the window. Suddenly he felt so young and overwhelmed. There was so much that he didn't know or understand. He felt like he'd just been flung into the deep end without ever being taught how to swim. It really would be nice to have someone that he could lean on.

He wished he could go back to how he was before the wedding. He was normally never so emotional. He had been content flitting from party to party and chasing both money and pleasure.

Well... no. That wasn't exactly true. He had told himself he was content, but he really had been searching for *more* hadn't he? Keiko was right.

But what did that even mean?

"Look, I'm not saying that we have to have some sort of dramatic reunion where you're brought in like some sort of lost sheep. I'm just saying, I'm here for you right now, and if you cracked open the door even slightly, I bet Ma would be there for you in an instant."

Bryant was tempted to just sit there, processing everything that had happened, but his mouth was moving before he even really thought about it.

"I'm not so sure I deserve support. Maybe there's a reason

I've never gotten on with our oh-so-perfect family. Maybe I am just like a cancer."

"Bryant, that isn't true."

He just shrugged, and his brother sighed.

"Look, I'm not going to pretend you're some sort of saint, and I'm sorry for hesitating before, but you're not a bad person," Bradley said.

"I'm beginning to think that the evidence indicates otherwise." He closed his eyes and thought back to all the letters from Ma that he ignored. He thought of how he had chosen a college far away from everyone and did not keep it a secret that he wasn't going to be stagnant and backwater like the rest of them.

He'd wanted to hurt them, so he did. He used people, women especially, and his entire life was built around accruing more and more wealth.

When was the last time he had helped someone, without expecting something in return? When had he ever created joy? Not an adrenaline rush, not a fulfillment of an addiction, not fueling greed, but pure, unadulterated *joy*.

He thought he was better than people like Keiko, who believed in some invisible guy in the sky and spent so much of their time trying to preach to people. And who could blame him considering all the mega-churches there were and how the Christians that got the most screen time in media were always the ones filled with hate and ignorance?

It was a mess. He was a mess.

Bradley spoke up, "Really? Because I see it differently. You've come to every engagement party and wedding of our brothers even though they make you miserable. I've seen the backhanded comments you get, and I'm sorry I never stood up for you, but I always admired how you would just brush them off instead of causing a real row.

"I remember when Bart was first hospitalized. You spent an entire week with him in the hospital along with Ma and Pa. You and Bart never got on even when you were younger, but you didn't care.

"When we were kids you would help me run my lines, letting me go over and over them until I was sure I had it one hundred percent perfect. You were always the best at bottle feeding any of the little runts that got rejected on the farm, especially the kittens. Everyone told you it was a waste, and that they were sick, and there was a reason their mama rejected them, but you didn't care.

"You've got flaws, little brother. You can be selfish, and you have a bad temper. For as brilliant as you are, you're short-sighted and take things personally way more than you should. But you were there for Keiko when she needed you. You stepped up for her and called me, even though the last time we'd talked you'd been struck for your effort.

"Now, you tell me, does that sound like something a *bad* person would do?"

Bryant was quiet for a long, long moment, Bradley's words washing over him in a torrent. If he could ever count on someone to give it to him straight, it was his math-minded bigger brother.

It was embarrassing, but he could feel tears welling up to his eye line. "You really believe all that?" he asked, almost afraid to speak. He didn't like showing weakness, but he felt he might crumble at any moment. He'd built his empire on what amounted to be sand, and the foundation was indeed shaking.

"I wouldn't say it if I didn't. There's an amazing, loving man in there, I know it. He's just been buried under a lot of hurt. I should have stood up for you more when we were younger. But I was a coward. At the time, I appreciated that the family seemed to begrudgingly accept that one of their sons liked putting on costumes and singing in front of an audience, so I didn't want to rock the boat.

"You had to defend yourself on your own and that taught you that you could only count on you. I'm sorry. But, if you're ready, I'd like to start over going forward. None of this black sheep or prodigal son stuff. I love you, brother, and I don't want all our lectures to chase you away."

Bryant didn't know what to say to that, he just nodded. It felt like his throat was swollen closed, and his eyes burned. When was the last time that he had cried? He couldn't remember. It was like he had sustained himself for so long on all the fluff and excitement and adrenaline that his body and mind didn't know how to handle a headier emotion.

He really had such a hollow existence, didn't he?

"Anyways, it's not something that you have to answer now. You've had a kinda intense day. How about we go in and make sure everything's taken care of? Seems like it's a good walk back to the front of the building."

Bryant nodded, so glad his brother understood that he just needed to think. To digest. To come to a decision on his own.

"All right. I'm gonna grab some bottles of water from the cooler in the back then we'll head out."

They did exactly that, walking in the quiet as Bryant turned things this way and that in his mind. By the time they reached the reception area, he didn't have any answers, but he did feel like he was on more solid ground.

They went up to the receptionist, and Bradley took care of all the talking. She told them that Keiko was currently in admittance, and they could take a seat to wait for an update if they liked.

So they did. They sat, and Bryant thought while Bradley worked on a sudoku puzzle on his phone.

Time ticked on and it was about an hour later that Dani came out, looking quite worn. When had she even gotten into town? Had it really been a month since the wedding?

"Hey," Bradley said, rising to his feet. "How is everything? Is she okay?"

"Yeah, I've never seen her this bad, but she's in good hands now. She admitted herself voluntarily, and she's gonna spend a few days here."

The short woman crossed over to Bryant, and unlike his interaction with Missy, instead of slapping him, she pulled him into a hug.

"Thank you so much for being there for my friend. What you did to help her means a lot to me."

Bryant awkwardly returned the gesture, completely blind-sided by it, but it wasn't unwelcome. When they parted, Dani was wiping tears from the corners of her eyes.

"It's getting pretty late. I'd like to go home and cuddle with my husband."

Bradley nodded. "I'm sure he's worried. Hey, Bryant. Why don't you come home? Like, really come home?"

It was tempting, even with the jumbled mess of thoughts and emotions in his mind, but in the end, he shook his head. "No. I know where I'm supposed to be right now. It's here with Keiko. I want to make sure she's okay."

"Are... are you sure?"

Yeah, he was. For once, he was in the right place at the right time, and he was going to do the right thing.

15

Keiko

*W*hen Keiko woke up, it was like she was emerging from a terrible, insidious nightmare that had lasted for days. Things were foggy and it seemed like her brain had been soaked in sludge, but at least she felt more like herself.

Looking around, she expected to see the pale mint pastels of her room. Mint had always been a good color, a soothing color, so she'd painted it the first thing when she'd moved into her new place. But she quickly realized that she wasn't home at all.

Oh, right. She'd checked herself into the psychiatry center her therapist helped run. The details were buried in her head, but she was sure that if she thought hard enough about it, she could recall the why and how of what all happened.

But first, she definitely needed to go to the bathroom. She must have been out for quite a while judging by the urgency of it, so she hurriedly shuffled out of her bed and over to the only other door of her room.

Grabbing the knob, she turned it to go in, but something held her in place. She didn't open it right. Letting go, she grabbed it again and turned.

No. Not right.

She turned it to the other side. Then the other. But no matter what she did, it just wasn't *right*.

Her bladder was throbbing, and she was sure that she was going to wet herself, when a knock sounded at the door and a nurse came in.

"Hey there, Miss Albryte. I'm Mackenzie, I'll be on shift today until Olivia takes over at eight."

"Oh, uh, nice to meet you."

"Yes, we'll talk later. But you have a visitor right now. Would you like me to let them in or do you need a bit more rest to settle in?"

It had to be Dani. Keiko's heart warmed, and she couldn't think of a better idea. "Yeah, let them in. I'm just gonna use the facilities."

"All right, sounds good dear."

She disappeared back out the door, and Keiko went about relieving herself and washing her face. Memories started to float back to her, mostly being held by Dani, her best friend humming to her, but when she emerged from the small bathroom, it wasn't Dani who was waiting for her at all.

"Bryant?" Keiko asked, completely taken aback. The last thing she remembered, he'd vomited all down her front, drenching her in warm acidic liquid.

And it was *chunky*.

"Hey there," he said, arms full of bags so he wasn't able to wave. "I brought you some stuff. Mind if I set them down?"

"...okay."

She watched as he crossed over to the small side table and set all of his bags down. Something about his movement was familiar, and she had a brief flash of him crouched in front of her in the kitchen.

Oh, goodness gracious.

He had been there.

More detail flooded back to her in sharp relief, and she recalled exactly what had happened.

She'd jumped into the shower, clothes and all, scrubbing herself with the hottest water possible. Her skin had instantly turned red, but it wasn't enough.

It was only after she was thoroughly soaked that she was able to pull her clothes off and chuck them in the corner of the tub. From there, she poured her body wash down her form and tried to free herself from every bit of grossness that was on her.

It was an uncontrollable compulsion. She needed to clean, clean, clean, *clean*. But no matter how much she scoured herself, she didn't get the relief of cleanliness. There was no relief, only more pressure to do. To scrub.

She stayed in there until the water had grown cold and her body wash ran out. She still had the feeling of creepy crawlies all over her body. She had forced herself out of the shower, but she'd suddenly realized that her apartment was absolutely filthy.

And then she'd fallen into the spiral, hook line and sinker.

Goodness, what would have happened if Bryant hadn't been there to call for help? She hadn't had a breakdown like that since her freshman year of college when all the stress and a resurgence of her eating disorder had combined to send her into a full OCD meltdown.

She was supposed to be stronger than that, yet here she was, watching as Bryant started to unload bags.

"What are you doing?"

"Oh, I just figured I'd bring you some essentials." A bottle of hand sanitizer came out first. Then latex gloves. "I know this place is probably real clean, but I figured it might make you feel extra sure if you could do it yourself." Next came some baby wipes, some dusting rags, hand soap, lotion. It was a *lot* of stuff.

She watched him, just standing in the bathroom doorway, until finally the entire table was covered with various cleaning and hygienic supplies. It had to have cost a pretty penny, but he was acting like it was perfectly normal.

Eventually, he finished and turned to talk to her. Or at least she assumed he was trying to talk to her because his mouth opened and closed, but no words came out.

Did he pity her? She didn't need it. Sure, she was sick, but she would get better. She had done it before, and she would do it again.

The tension built up quickly, becoming more awkward until finally Keiko spoke.

"Why are you doing this?"

He shrugged. "I dunno. Figured I owed you. Or something. Thanks, by the way."

"For what?"

"For coming and getting me just because my brother asked you to. That was... you didn't have to do that."

Oh, that wasn't what she expected. "You needed help."

"Yeah, yeah, I really did."

The conversation stilled, petering out until the awkwardness started to grow again. Clearing his throat, Bryant looked to the door.

"Uh, I'll get out of your hair. I know I'm probably the last person you want to see right now."

Was that true? She didn't feel like it was.

"No, it's okay," she said quickly. "I, uh, I think I'd rather not be alone right now."

"Okay."

He crossed over to the singular chair by the bed, and she sat on the mattress. Normally she tried not to do non-bedtime activities where she was supposed to sleep because it made it difficult to get a full night's rest, but she didn't see how she had much of a choice.

Once more they were quiet, neither of them seeming to know how to start the conversation. She was still in a state of disbelief that he was even there. She had been almost certain that things had broken beyond repair between them, and that was only reinforced by the fact that she had completely lost her marbles right in front of him.

After a while, she figured it was probably her who should lead the conversation.

"I bet you're wondering what happened," she said flatly, nerves and embarrassment bubbling in her gut.

He shrugged again. "I don't need to know if it's private. Things happen."

"Yeah, and that was definitely a thing, to put it mildly." She chuckled, but the sound was fake even to her own ears. "I, uh, I've got some mental health stuff that I usually have handled, but you saw a severe episode. What happens when I don't take care of me."

He shifted again, and she could tell he was uncomfortable. That was the reason she usually was so private with what was going on with her. People either judged her or didn't understand or thought she was making it up. It was one of the reasons it had taken her so long to get help.

"That's an awful nice way of you tiptoeing around how I pushed you there."

"Pardon?" Keiko asked, staring at him with wide eyes.

"Look, I'm not proud of what I said to you in that restaurant. I realize that hanging out with someone like me was probably pretty bad for you, but you did it anyway. You're a bigger person than me. And although I didn't get sick on you on purpose, you wouldn't have been put into that position if you hadn't driven all the way to that club to save me from a bender.

"So I don't blame you if you never want to see me again. I... I probably shouldn't have even come here, but I wanted to make sure you were all right." He grimaced. "Well, as all right as you can be considering the situation."

If there was a list of all the things in the world that Keiko thought could have possibly happened, that was right about at the end of the list next to the man growing wings and flying into space.

"It's not your fault."

"Keiko, you don't need to try to soften the blow. I can take responsibility for my actions."

She shook her head. "No, you don't understand. I'm not trying to sugarcoat anything. It's literally not your fault."

He looked so vulnerable when his eyes flicked to her. "I... don't understand."

"Look, I'm not going to lie to you and pretend that you didn't exacerbate it, but the truth is I'm sick, and I am responsible for my own health. There are highs and lows, flares and recessions, and the most random of things can trigger a slide."

"I... see?"

She could tell that he wasn't quite getting it, but he didn't look disbelieving or annoyed, so she decided she might as well tell him everything.

"Look, so I have OCD. You've probably heard of it before, it's in the movies and on TV enough, but it's not represented very well. It's basically a combination of obsessions, compulsions and intrusive thoughts. Sometimes I just get this... urge, I guess you'd call it, and they can sometimes be impossible to ignore.

"So, I develop these rituals that are supposed to relieve the obsession. They're not something I consciously do, but it's like these random two points of data my brain collects. Let's say maybe I'm obsessing over the height of all my books and how they don't line up to make an even plane. Instead of just accepting that books come in different sizes, my brain will say that if I don't get them in order, the entire house will burn down and the only way to stop it is to fix the books."

"Really? Your house will burn down?" he didn't say it critically, more with surprise or concern, which gave her the courage to keep going.

"Yeah. Some of them aren't as direct. Like if I don't turn on and off the water three times, acid will spray out instead. Or that if I don't lock my door exactly ten times, someone will break in."

"So it's kinda like, step on a crack, break your mama's back?"

Keiko nodded eagerly. She hadn't expected him to understand. "Yes, that's exactly it. My brain will just tell me things like that, and I either have to do a ritual or break the cycle to keep functioning.

"But sometimes the rituals don't relieve the obsession, and that's where I can run into trouble. That's also kind of what you witnessed, but it was exacerbated by a whole lot of energy drinks, staying awake for over twenty-four hours, and freaking out over the whole..." she gestured to him and made a gagging sound.

"Right. Okay. I got you. Sorry about that, still."

"Thank you, I appreciate it."

"So, is that why you eat, uh, a little differently?" he asked cautiously. "Because of the OCD?"

"Kinda. I, uh, I also struggled with anorexia when I was younger. I've been in recovery for a while now, but it can be difficult to manage when my OCD is acting up. Textures or flavors of food, sometimes even colors will set me off."

He nodded, looking like he was digesting it all. "Huh. I knew a lot about depression, and I studied PTSD when my brother came home, but this sounds a lot different than that."

Huh, he studied when his brother came home? That was... sweet. A lot of people wouldn't go that far for other people.

"Yeah, there's a lot of different mental illnesses that affect people in different ways. For a long time I thought that I wasn't ever going to be able to have a life. That I was going to have to live with my parents forever and never amount to much.

"But then I went to this church retreat when I was sixteen, and I suddenly had this peace."

"Is that how you got involved in the church?"

She nodded. "Yeah. Being there brings me a lot of peace. Usually, at least. It's not like a magical panacea that can just make me healthy in a snap, but it helps, you know? It's like a support, and knowing that I'm not alone really does help."

"Huh, wish I could get that kind of comfort from it."

"Have you ever tried?"

He huffed. "Ma and Pa dragged me off to church for eighteen years of my life. Yeah, I'd say I tried."

Ugh, Keiko understood the resentment in his voice. She personally felt that children didn't benefit from sermons in the same way adults did, and forcing them to sit through something they didn't understand week after week just made a kid associate God with unpleasant things. It was one of the reasons

she had pushed so much for age-appropriate Sunday School
and Vacation Bible Studies. Learning about God should be fun
and relevant to children.

"That's not what I mean. I meant have you ever just tried to
sit with God, on your own terms, and just... talk, I guess? Sort
out what you're feeling and what questions you might have for
him? You know, bring your grievances to light?"

"I... No. I haven't. I can't even really name the last time I
slowed down enough to do that."

"It might be something you want to try, you know, if you get
your feet under you. How are you feeling, by the way?"

"Hah, don't you think it's ironic to be worrying about me
right now considering the situation?"

Coming from most people, that definitely would have been
an insult. But with the way he cracked a bashful smile at her,
and his eyes sparkled, she couldn't help but chuckle.

"Fair enough. I suppose I do have a habit of trying to take
care of other people instead of focusing on myself."

"So I heard. Apparently, it's even in your notes."

"I'm sorry, what now?"

He flushed. "Oh, should I not have said that? It's just, uh,
when I called the number you told me to call and they walked
me through getting you here, they mentioned a way to get you
to do things was to phrase it as if you were helping me. Don't
you remember?"

She closed her eyes and tried to recall, but the past day was
still in bits and splotches all through her mind. They were
puzzle pieces, all right, and she was still finding which ones
went where.

"Not really. But boy, that's embarrassing."

"Really? I don't think so."

"Why's that?"

"Think about it. When some people are drunk, inebriated or stressed, they'll hurt other people or be snappish and mean. But you, when you're sick and at your weakest, just want to help people. If that's not a pretty big indication of what kind of person you are, I don't know what is."

She felt herself flush as well. "You make me sound much more noble than I am."

"Maybe, or maybe you're just not the best judge of it. It's hard to be objective when it comes to yourself, isn't it?"

He was smiling at her, and she was smiling at him, and it was possibly the most genuine conversation they'd ever had. Narrowing her eyes, she gave him a dramatically suspicious look.

"Why, if I didn't know better, I would think that you were saying I was a good person."

"Well, you're certainly not on anyone's naughty list."

"That you know of."

He chuckled. "If anyone knows about naughty lists and how to get on them, it's me."

"I suppose. But the good things about those lists is it's not permanent. You can leave them at any time."

"Right, because it's just so easy."

"It could be."

She hadn't meant to say that so earnestly, but it was enough to halt the conversation as the two of them shared a meaningful look. It was strangely intense, and she wasn't sure exactly what she was trying to communicate to him, but it definitely felt like they were saying *something* to each other.

But just as quickly as the moment appeared, it was popped as an orderly knocked on the door.

"Ms. Albryte?"

"Uh, yeah, come in."

This time it wasn't Mackenzie who came in, but instead a tall orderly. "I hope I'm not interrupting, but it's time for your check-in with Dr. Hyleir and then lunch."

Keiko nodded. "What diet do they have me on?"

"Right now, just the BRAT one, but I'm sure once you talk to Dr. Hyleir, she'll get you back onto something more calorie-heavy."

Keiko made a face. "Good. I hate the BRAT diet."

"What's the BRAT diet?" Bryant asked.

"Bananas, rice, applesauce, and toast," Keiko answered quickly. "But I hate the texture of applesauce so it's mostly just a BRT diet for me."

"Yeah, but it doesn't quite have the same ring to it, does it?" the orderly asked with a laugh.

"Nope."

"I guess I better get going," Bryant said, standing up and striding toward the door.

Keiko hadn't expected to be upset by the thought of him taking his leave. She had been enjoying the conversation so much and how for once it didn't seem like they were playing some sort of complicated game of chess or cat and mouse.

The youngest Miller son stopped just in front of the orderly, however, and shot Keiko an uncertain look. "I can come and keep you company tomorrow. That is, if you would like that, of course."

A strange sort of weightlessness flickered in Keiko's chest, so she nodded before finding her voice. "Yeah, I would like that."

"You can count on it then. Text me if you get cleared for regular food and I'll try to bring us some lunch."

"Sounds good to me."

Bryant gave Keiko a warm smile before he left. And at that, she felt her heart flutter.

16

Keiko

"*H*ello, Keiko. I'm sorry you haven't been having a very good time of late. Are you ready to talk about it?"

Keiko didn't answer right away, instead taking a long sip of the water she had been given. The therapy room that she was in was familiar. She'd spent plenty of hours sitting on the velvety couch, finding comfort and wisdom with the doctor, but somehow it felt like everything had changed.

Maybe she was the one who changed.

Was she changing? She didn't really know.

"It hasn't been the easiest time."

"I can imagine. Do you want to summarize for me what happened? We have a vague idea from the gentleman who helped bring you to us, but not much else. When you came in last night, you weren't in a very good state. Do you have any idea what got you into that position?"

"Well, I've kind of been struggling for the past few months. With the way the world is going now, and all the hate, and all the ignorance, it's been hard not to feel like everything is going downhill."

"I understand. A lot of people have been having issues with those particular subjects. But something tells me that that's not what set you off, Ms. Albryte. You've always had such a strong support system, and your faith helps you as well; I imagine that it might have taken a litany of things to bring you to that position."

That was the thing about Dr. Hyleir; she always was perceptive. Keiko had heard horror stories about people who ended up with disrespectful or disbelieving doctors who ended up hurting them instead of helping them. But Dr. Hyleir wasn't that way.

"Well... no. I sort of took on this project."

"Oh, a project? You normally do so well with those."

"Yeah, I guess I do but..."

"You're hesitating, which usually means it's something you don't want to admit. Is it something you feel guilty about, Keiko?"

"Maybe. A little."

"Why don't you tell me about it then."

"I... okay. You know how I talk about the Millers a lot?"

"Yes, I believe two of them are your emergency contacts. The mother and one of the brothers?"

"Yes, that's them."

"Why do you bring them up?"

"Well... my project was basically their younger son."

Dr. Hyleir raised one of her meticulously sculpted eyebrows. "Would you care to elaborate?"

"I suppose that's necessary. You see, he, uh... he's not like the other Millers."

"What do you mean by that exactly?"

"Well, they all stayed in town and they're all involved in the church one way or the other. They're good examples of what Christians should be. You know, loving and kind. Sure, they make mistakes the same as anybody else, but at their core, you can tell they're good people."

"And this youngest son, he's not a good people?"

Keiko felt a jolt of alarm. "Oh, no! He is. I think. It's just, I... I suppose the best way to put it is that he's kind of... lost."

"Lost?"

"He's not Christian, and while I understand that is a choice that people are free to make, it doesn't feel like a choice for him. More like something that's been forced on him."

"That's interesting, why do you believe that?"

"I don't know, it's just a feeling that I get. He's a complex person. There's this outer layer that's confident and smarmy and superior, but it really seems to be a front."

"Are you certain of that?" she asked dutifully. "Sometimes we like to imagine that we find good traits within people, or reasons for why they act how they act, but the reality is their outer self really is their true self. There's no mystery, or layers."

"I understand that," Keiko said. She could think of at least ten different people like that. "But that's not the case here. I can tell that he's wounded under there, and he's one of those wounded people who reacts by lashing out. But he's kind, and smart, and surprisingly thoughtful when he manages to get his head out of his own ego."

"If I didn't know better, I would think that you might have feelings for this young son."

Keiko sat up stock straight. What? Feelings?

Did she have feelings for Bryant?

She sat there a moment, thinking. Turning the idea over and over in her head. She analyzed, reanalyzed, and then did it again.

"I suppose that is possible."

"Possible?"

"I hadn't thought about it until you brought it up. And I think possibly I could be developing feelings for him. But also... I'm not sure that I can feel that way about anyone."

"And why is that?"

She shrugged. "Just because it feels like there's not a lot of room in my head or in my heart. I've got the church and my friends and my family, and I'm thinking of getting my masters in library science so I can find a full-time job somewhere.

"Maybe, *maybe*, I could squeeze someone in. But they'd have to be the perfect someone. Someone I got along with and who helped me grow as a person and in my faith."

"And do you think this young man could be someone like that?"

"I don't know. Maybe?" She took a deep breath and tried to think about it. "But probably not."

"I see. I think that it's exciting that you may or may not be feeling emotions you never had time for previously. That's just a normal part of growing up."

"Dr. Hyleir, I'm twenty-six, not sixteen. I've been an adult for quite a while."

"Even adults have plenty of growing to do." She cleared her throat. "So tell me, what was the nature of your project with this young man."

Keiko grimaced. Now that she had to explain it to a medical professional, she was acutely aware of how ridiculous and sketchy her plan sounded. "For the lack of a better word, I wanted to fix him."

"Fix him?"

"Yeah, you know, reconnect him with his family. Bring him to God. Make him ditch the high-flying lifestyle for something more fulfilling."

"And you feel that you have the authority to do something like that?"

"At the time I didn't think of it as something I needed authority to do. My plan wasn't to bluster into his life like some hand of God and tell him what to do. I just thought if I hung around him, I could lead by example. If I could show him the amazing things that could come your way when you trust in God, and if I planted little seeds of hope and wisdom, maybe he'd come around."

"I see. After hearing yourself say it out loud, do you see any sort of issues with how that comes across?"

Keiko sighed. "Yeah. It sounds like I'm trying to change him."

"I would agree with that. And maybe we shouldn't always expect someone to change if they don't want to change themselves."

"But, maybe we can be a good influence to someone to help them see there's a better way of life."

"This is true, and there is a possibility of that happening. But we've also got to get you to a place where you won't let it affect you so if you can't help him like you'd like to. Do you think perhaps your conscience was objecting to you trying to change him and that could have helped trigger this most recent episode?"

"That sounds logical to me."

"All right. And do you think that was all that triggered you?"

"Most of it, at least."

"Most of it?"

Keiko found herself once again in the insightful gaze of her doctor. Goodness, the therapist really knew how to look right through a person.

"Is there anything you've left out?"

If Keiko was anybody else, she might have squirmed in her seat. But as it was, she just frowned slightly and felt that squirmy feeling all over her skin. "We may have gotten into a fight."

"Oh, really?"

Keiko nodded.

"And how did that go? Did you scream at each other? Call each other names?"

"No, no, nothing like that. In fact, the whole thing was pretty quiet because it was in a restaurant. No one even turned their heads."

"I see. So not your standard fight. But obviously it impacted you if you're bringing it up now. What happened?"

"He said some pointed words to me."

"Such as?"

"Nothing I haven't heard before. That I'm a control freak. That I'm obsessed with calories and my weight. You know, standard stuff that someone who doesn't know about my illness might just throw around."

"And yet it bothered you."

"...yeah, yeah it did."

"Is there a particular reason why?"

Keiko shifted, trying to remember why his words had cut right through her to her heart. "He might have also said that I was obsessed with how others saw me, so that was why I had my calm and collected facade to appear superior when really I'm just as ordinary and shallow as everyone else around me."

"Huh, those *are* some very pointed words. And this is the man you call sweet?"

"I said he could be sweet. In that moment he was hurt and angry with some things I had said to him, and he was trying to bring me down to his level. I understand why it happened."

"But knowing the reason for something doesn't necessarily excuse it."

"I know, and I'm not excusing it. We'll have a talk about it later. We haven't really had a chance since, you know."

She nodded. "I'm glad you know that's unacceptable and have set up that boundary. So maybe, instead, we should focus on why those words bothered you. Do you worry you're just like everyone else around you? And if you were, would that be such a bad thing?"

Would it? Keiko felt her teeth set to her lip, and she realized that her index finger was rubbing in specific circles against the fabric of the couch.

"I... I don't know."

"Actually, I think you do have an idea of what the answer is, but you don't want to say it because you don't want to sound arrogant, or prideful. Remember, this is a safe, closed-off space here, Keiko. You can tell me things that you wouldn't other people, even if you think it makes you look bad or selfish."

There were a few more moments of tug of war within herself. "I guess yes would be the answer. It's not that I think I'm better than everyone, I don't. I happen to be smart and insightful, but that doesn't comment on my character.

"But it's just that, ever since I was young, I felt like I was destined for greater things. Like I had a purpose beyond football games, or going to prom, or buying a house and settling down. I thought I was called by God to change the world."

"And do you no longer feel that way?"

"No, I still feel that way, but he made me wonder if the only reason I felt that way was because I had some sort of holy superiority complex. Some chosen-by-God delusion or something."

Dr. Hyleir didn't answer, tapping her foot lightly, and Keiko felt her confidence sag.

"I... don't seem like I have that, do I?"

"No, I don't think you're delusional or have a Saint complex. But I think, perhaps, you've forgotten how important something small can be."

"I don't catch your drift."

"You've heard of the butterfly effect, yes?"

"Uh, yes. A butterfly flaps its wings in China and causes a hurricane in California, meaning that you never know the consequences of your actions and even the littlest things can end up doing a lot."

"Good. Okay, now imagine this. What if you've already done many of the great things you were supposed to?"

Keiko blinked at her. "Uh, excuse me?"

"I understand I don't know every facet of your life, but from what you've told me, you've done some pretty incredible things."

Keiko made a dismissive sound. "Putting out bagels and running Bible studies isn't exactly going to revolutionize the world."

"No, but if I recall right, weren't Chastity and Ben on the outs when you helped them reconcile?"

"Yeah, they give me some credit for that."

"And Chastity has gone on to become a successful online

personality, which has allowed her to go on mission and relief trips across the world, correct?"

"... I suppose that's true."

"And what about your friend Dani?"

"What about her?"

"She struggles with depression, and you encouraged her to seek help for that, right?"

"I mean, it helped that I've been in therapy since I was a teen. It made it less scary for her."

"And would you say it was because of that encouragement that she received, they were able to continue their relationship, which led them all the way up to being married?"

Keiko was beginning to see the path Dr. Hyleir was laying out, and it was making her uncomfortable. "There could be a correlation there."

"And I believe you told me that the Touhey farm has become much more successful since Bradley's been helping with their investments and finances. And also, that one of her brothers is working with an inner-city program to rebuild homes damaged from arson while the other is a firefighter for the town."

"Yeah, that whole chapter of their lives definitely fueled some big life changes. Money was so tight before that they never would have had time to volunteer or be off their ranch for so long."

"So let's take this young man you're trying to 'help.' Let's say you're able to unite him with his family. What kind of changes do you think that could wrought?"

"Wrought is a very strange word to use."

"Don't deflect. I want you to think about it. I was able to bring up those instances quickly. Would it be fair to say that there are probably even more instances, ones that I don't know about? Ones that even you don't know about?"

"I..." Keiko swallowed. "I've never thought of it like that."

"Perhaps you should. I understand that you and I have different faiths, but I understand what it feels like to be called by a purpose, even a destiny as some people say. But what I'd like you to consider is that it's not some grand battle, or perhaps a revolution, or even rescuing a baby from a burning building.

"There is an incalculable value in the gifts you have brought your friends. You've given them support, put them on paths to get help, aided them in making decisions that led them, in some cases, to their soulmate.

"And let's say you are able to help the young man. And I say *help*, not fix. You and I both know how inherently toxic it is to view people as objects that are broken or assume that they're 'fixable.'"

"Yeah, definitely. That is burned into my head quite deeply by now."

"Good. So, again, let's say you are able to help this Miller son and he reunites with his family. Maybe they go on to do great things together. Maybe he puts his wealth to good use. Donates to a charity. The possibilities for good are endless, all of which would happen because of *you*."

Keiko felt goosebumps rise along her arms at the idea. "That is a pretty heavy conclusion to come to."

"It is, but I think it is one that has merit. It is possible he could want to become a better person, with your influence. But you can't expect to change someone. And you need to be sure you see him for what he really is, whatever that may be." She paused and looked at her watch. "Goodness. It's hard to believe that it's almost been an hour. Would you like to take a break and then meet up again in the afternoon, or would you prefer to rest more and try to work on things tomorrow?"

"I think... I think I would prefer to meet tomorrow. You've given me a lot to think about, and I'm very tired."

"Yes, I do remember that you tend to have a strong and long reaction to sedatives. We did give you some yesterday to help you on intake. You won't receive those again unless you start having night terrors or issues sleeping."

Keiko nodded. "Okay. That sounds good to me. Thank you, Dr. Hyleir."

"Of course, Keiko. Just remember that you're not alone in this, no matter what it might seem like."

"Yeah. I do remember that. Most of the time."

17

Bryant

*H*e looked down at the large bag of food he had brought, wondering if he had gone overboard, but he had no idea what was appropriate and what wasn't. Maybe Keiko had a mini-fridge and she could put any leftovers in there?

He didn't know, and he found himself wishing that he'd asked Dani more questions during their short talk on the phone that morning. He'd been smart enough to enquire about if she had any allergies and her food preferences—which had been a very long and particular list—but now he was kicking himself for not getting enough details.

He walked into the entrance and was glad to see the same receptionist as the day before. She waved him back, saying that Keiko had already informed her he was on his way.

That morning, when he had woken up, he had almost

expected Keiko to ask him not to return. But instead she'd told him that her BRAT diet had indeed been lifted, and she was good to eat all her favorite foods again.

He knocked on her door and this time it was Keiko who answered, already looking much better than she had the previous day. The dark circles under her eyes were gone, her hair was clean and brushed back into a low braid, and she was dressed in a soft sundress that looked so pretty and bright against her pale skin.

"Hey there," she said, smiling at him in a way that made his heart jump. It wasn't a feeling he was accustomed to, but he didn't really mind it.

"Hey," he said right back, lifting his bag of food. "I brought you lunch."

"And lunch for a whole army too."

He scoffed. "It's not *that* big."

"I am well aware that perhaps I have a skewed perception of what is or isn't a lot of food, but I'm pretty sure I could do a whole weight training regimen with that bag."

"You may have a point."

She stepped to the side, allowing him in, and he shuffled past her to the table. Perhaps it was strange, but it filled his chest with pride when he saw that she had taken all the cleaning supplies that he had brought and put it into different places in her room.

"I'm sure that if you have any leftovers, some of the nurses and workers will be happy to take care of them for you."

"I bet. The cafeteria here is terrible, and the food places around have incredibly long lines."

"And I thought this place was supposed to help you feel better, not drive you crazy."

Keiko made a sort of choking sound at that.

Bryant felt his stomach drop. Should he have not said that?

Keiko spoke up, "You know, that would make a great sort of insurance conspiracy. I can see it in headlines now, local clinic found out to steadily drive patients mad in the hopes of getting more money."

Thank goodness, she didn't take it poorly. He needed to think more about what he was saying and who he was saying it to.

"Don't get me started on conspiracy theories. I hear some crazy ones," he said.

"Oh, I didn't know that casinos were rife with theorists."

"Not that. You know my business is more than the one casino I own. There's a large online element, and you'd be amazed at what you can stumble onto there."

"Your tone tells me that's not a good thing," Keiko said.

"Yeah, well even people living under a rock know that the internet is full of all sorts of dark places."

"Ah, and is that where you think I live? Under a rock?"

He drew in his breath to object before seeing the slight curve to her mouth. "You're messing with me."

"Am I?"

"All right, all right, tease all you want. What would you like first? I've got a plain burger with no sauce or drippage, only extra cheese. I got you some buttered noodles from that one Italian place Dani said you liked and sushi from... I forget the name of the restaurant."

"Wow, Bryant, this is a lot of stuff."

"I know, I know. But just tell me which one you'd like so I look less like I went overboard when someone comes in."

"All right. Give me the sushi first. That will be a good appetizer."

"Sounds like a plan. I'm guessing you'll want some chopsticks?"

"Why, because I'm Asian?"

He blinked at her owlishly, the platter of sushi frozen in the air.

To her credit, she managed to hold her poker face for quite a few beats before breaking into a peal of laughter. "Yes, I'd like the chopsticks, please."

"I suppose I deserved that."

"It was pretty fun to watch your face."

"Well laugh it up. I'm sure you'll be singing my praises once you taste all this good food."

"Ugh, you wouldn't want to hear me sing. I couldn't carry a tune in a bucket."

"What? There's something that the amazing and intelligent Keiko can't do?"

"We are sitting in a mental institution because I had a break down from a disorder that literally prevents me from doing normal, everyday things."

"You, uh, may have a point there."

"Yeah, you bet I do."

Bryant watched as she effortlessly picked up a piece of sushi between the two sticks then popped the entire thing into her mouth. He watched her chew methodically for quite a while, then as she swallowed, and it traveled down the smooth, pale column of her throat.

She really was *beautiful*, wasn't she? From her thick lashes to her full lips to her shoulders to the soles of her feet. Sure, she was delicate, and a lot of her features were fine, but there was an iron sort of strength to her. Something unbreakable and forged in fire.

He admired that. Sometimes he felt like he was so rootless

that the strongest of winds would carry him away. It wasn't a very good feeling, so he wasn't sure if he was jealous or admired her.

Maybe both.

"You're staring at me."

He startled, averting his eyes away. "Oh, sorry. I didn't realize."

"What, do I have wasabi on my face?"

"I, uh, I don't know how to say it without sounding rude."

She set her chopsticks down and looked him in the eyes. "After my talk with Dr. Hyleir, I realize that not being honest with myself helped set me off this time, so I'd prefer if we tried to keep everything as truthful as possible."

He swallowed, but if she wanted honesty, he would give her just that. He was at the point where she could probably ask him to throw himself off a cliff and he would. Not that he was suicidal, or anything, but he trusted Keiko enough to know she would have to have a good reason to ask him to do anything like that.

"Okay. I was just thinking that I was surprised you were able to take a whole bite like that."

"Oh, is that all?" She let out a long breath.

Bryant wondered if she cared what he said. If he didn't know better, he would think so.

"Some sushi you can bite in half, but some of it is too messy. Since this has eel sauce on it—which I love—it's better to just pop it into my mouth."

"Huh, I see. So you've got eating down to a science then."

"That's the nicest way I've ever heard it put, but yes, you could say so. Recovery has been a long road, but it's given me plenty of time to figure out strategies to get through the day."

"I see. Sounds complicated."

"It can be, but who's life isn't? When you think about it. I just have some very specific hurdles I have to jump over."

"You're a very generous person, you know that?"

"Really? I don't think so. Just doing my part."

"I think you do more than that."

She didn't answer right away, instead taking another bite of sushi. "You're being awfully generous yourself with all those compliments."

"Haha, I'm not trying to. I just have a lot to make up for."

"Do you?"

Although the conversation was much more banter-filled than it had ever been before, it still somewhat felt like some sort of high stakes strategy game where every move was setting up for another move. Like they were cautiously circling each other, each afraid of hurting the other or being hurt.

"Yeah, look, I know there hasn't exactly been a great time to say this, but I really do apologize for what I said in that restaurant. I was wrong, and hateful, and I just want you to know that's not normally me." Wait, she wanted honesty. And if he was going to be honest with her, he needed to be honest with himself.

"Well, maybe it is me. I guess I don't handle criticism very well. It brings out an ugly side of me."

"Actually, I think you're excellent at handling criticism. You have to be, considering your line of work and all the comments I read online. I just think that there are specific things that you're insecure about and I managed to touch on some or all of them."

Bryant chuckled at that. "Pretty much all of them. I don't usually feel like I'm so easy to read, but you looked right through me."

"Like I said, I have a talent."

"You're not kidding me."

The conversation lulled as she ate more, and she made it through a few more pieces of sushi before switching over to her burger. It was comfortable, but it still felt like there was something lingering in the air between them, something that needed to be said or done.

He wished that he could just take an eraser to their meeting and do it all over again. That he approached her as a human and an equal instead of a conquest. But what was done was done, and these were consequences that he couldn't run away from.

Finally, she set her utensils down again. He figured that was her signal that she wanted to talk.

"Will you tell me something?" Keiko asked.

"Whatever you want," he agreed far too quickly.

"Whatever I want, that's a heady promise."

"Well, I'd prefer to keep my social security number secret, but I'm sure you'd have a good reason to need it."

"And what did I do to possibly earn that level of trust?"

"I... I don't know. I just know that I can. I mean, you did drive for four hours just to come get me from a club when I was blackout drunk."

"I'm not sure how smart that was considering the situation."

"True, but I sure am grateful."

"All right then. Can you tell me why you dislike your family so much?"

Bryant sucked in a breath. Of course, she had to ask that. "I was pretty sure I've said—"

"Hold on, I might not have phrased that clearly. There's a rift between you and them. I want to know the first moment that you ever remember knowing that it was there and being hurt by it."

"What?"

"I want to know what started it all. What put the first domino in place that led to the situation you have now."

"That's... that was a long time ago." Bryant felt the pleasant feeling start to fade. He supposed it was naïve to think that he could ever escape the presence of his family, but it had been nice to hope, for a moment, that it could have been just him and Keiko.

"But I know you know."

"Bold of you to assume."

"I'm not assuming." She narrowed her eyes. "For example, I don't know the *actual* first step of my developing an eating disorder, but I absolutely remember the first instance I consciously thought there was something wrong with my body. It's burned into my mind. I couldn't forget it even if I wanted to. It's a part of my history, woven into me like a tapestry."

Bryant paused to take a long drink, thinking over whether or not he could brush off her uncomfortable question. The problem was that answering her required him to delve deep into his mind, to a period of his life that he mostly sealed off due to all the bad memories.

But hadn't he promised she could ask anything? It wouldn't do for him to break his word already.

"All right, let me think a moment."

He closed his eyes and tried to recall. There were certain bigger moments that stuck out in his mind, burning points of hot coal, but there smaller moments that occurred before then.

Finally, he settled on it, his stomach dropping out and the bitter taste of rejection filling his mouth.

"All right. I think I've got it. I was eight, and for a while I got really into model building. I started with cars then planes then dinosaurs. I went through them like a speed demon and liked to paint them up nice and give them away as presents.

"I don't know if people actually liked them, but my aunts and uncles and older cousins always acted like it was the coolest thing. I remember one, Aunt Daisy, asked me to auto-graph it because she was so impressed."

Keiko nodded, clearly listening, so he continued. He hadn't talked about this ever, mostly because he thought it was silly. A child's view of the world. Interpreting something that wasn't a big deal like a trauma that felt so much worse.

Because compared to Keiko, he had it easy. In fact, he was feeling pretty ungrateful for acting like such a victim from time to time.

Not that he forgave his family. No, there was too much hurt and bitterness there. But he still felt ridiculous for letting himself be wounded so deeply by such incidents.

"Eventually, I went through all of those figurines from the site that we used, so we moved on to fantasy ones. Dragons and knights and all sorts of things. I loved them, even more than all the others, and I used my birthday money to buy this really elaborate one that was supposed to be an entire battlefield with this giant hydra.

"I was almost all the way done with it when my brothers came barreling into my room. It was winter, so they didn't want to go outside in the cold and were tossing a football in the house. Bart tripped, and the next thing we all knew, he crashed right into it.

"Everything was broken. Pieces smashed, even the table it was on cracked in two and went to the ground. It was a mess, but when Bart got up, he blamed *me* for having my 'stupid model' in the middle of the room."

"That sounds upsetting. And that's the moment that started it all?"

"No, not then. That was just brothers being brothers. And I suppose I've never had a very good temper, because I lost it. I jumped on him and bit him and scratched him all up. Ben ran over and pried me off while Benji held Bart off. As for Bradley, he ran and got Mom."

Bryant let out a chuckle at that.

"Looking back, it's interesting to think of it from her perspective. She was just feeding her chickens, and she comes inside to absolute mayhem in the sitting room.

"There was a whole lot of yelling and screaming, and eventually she managed to get the story out. She scolded and punished my brothers for running in the house and playing ball, but that wasn't enough for me. I was sobbing and screaming and generally throwing a *real* tantrum and finally, Ma looked to me and said I was being ridiculous; it was just a little model, a toy, and she would buy me a new one if it mattered that much.

"And that was when I knew that something so very important to me meant nothing to her. That she didn't care and thought it was replaceable. Later, when we were all getting ready for bed, Bart told me that I was a freak and an idiot for caring about my stupid dragons and things. My brothers all stood around, continuing to brush their teeth, and I could tell by their faces that they all agreed.

"So yeah, that was it. That was the moment that I realized they saw me as something other than them. Something that didn't belong." He felt his cheeks burn. "I bet that sounds real stupid, huh?"

Keiko shook her head. "No. It makes sense. It always starts

as something innocuous, something little that you're supposed to be able to 'get over,' but you never really do, do you?"

He shouldn't have even been surprised at that point, but he was. He hadn't expected her to understand or agree with him. "You sound like you have personal experience. Rough relationship with your parents?"

"No, my parents saved my life. They can be a smidge overbearing while at the same time being a touch unobservant. It was one of the ways I got away with so much when I was at my sickest."

Bryant tried to piece it together then, but he was baffled. "Then... what was your moment that made you feel different than everyone else?"

"Fifth grade Girl Scouts. I wasn't really much of one for group activities or anything that happened outside of a book, so I would usually just read to myself after my parents dropped me off. Closer to the end of the meeting, when the leaders were busy with other things, this group of girls surrounded me and asked if I ate cats or dogs and pulled at the corners of their eyes to make them slanted. That was the moment that I knew I wasn't like them, and I never would be."

Bryant sat back, trying to catch up with all the mental images that flashed through his mind. He could see it so clearly playing out in front of him, along with all the humiliation and rejection that probably had filled little Keiko for the first time.

"Geez, kids can be really cruel, huh?"

"I've found that adults can be too. Theirs is just more guided."

"Fair enough."

She switched to the noodles and ate a single one before giving him a soft smile. "Thank you for telling me that."

"No problem. Like I said, it's the least I could do."

"No, the least you could do is absolutely nothing at all. The important thing to remember is that you've at least tried to do the right thing."

"I'll... try to keep that in mind."

"I think you should."

She had slowed down in her eating, but Bryant finally felt settled enough to dig in himself. Thankfully, the conversation grew much more relaxed, and he could truly say he had a good time.

He just hoped Keiko did too.

18

Keiko

*S*he ended up staying three full days at the center with Dr. Hyleir before she felt comfortable enough to go home the next day. She was aware that she probably should have called her parents and told them what was going on, but she didn't want them to worry.

And her parents would *definitely* worry.

She had plenty to occupy her without them, however. Between her sessions with Dr. Hyleir, her quiet time spent in prayer and reflection, and her visits from Bryant and Dani, she had a pretty packed schedule.

And boy, had she learned quite a lot about Bryant in that short amount of time.

In just a few days, she was able to confirm a lot of what she had suspected. That he was kind. That he was creative. That he was a bit insecure and emotionally aware. That he loved animals and the act of creating something beautiful, and that he feared failure.

They shared so many similarities, the two of them. Two people who'd been shattered in the past and had found very different ways of gluing themselves together.

"Hey there, are you ready to go?"

She stood up as Bryant entered the lobby. Of course, Dani and Benji had volunteered to pick her up and take her back to her apartment as soon as she started talking about leaving. But when Bryant asked, looking at her through those thick lashes of his, a slight layer of dark stubble on his chiseled, tanned face, she'd agreed.

She didn't know what exactly had happened to the man, but he seemed... different to her. There was still that sort of rule-breaking naughtiness to him, but there was something else. Sometimes she caught him looking at her, not like a prize to be won, but like someone who was important to him.

Someone he admired.

It was so different from the lustful gazes he had used when they first met that she couldn't help but think if maybe, just maybe, Dr. Hyleir was right.

But even if the doctor was, Keiko needed time before she pursued that. She needed to heal and bolster up her health in all aspects before she considered anything like the possibility of a relationship.

What was that one saying in the Bible? Remove the log from her own eye before the splinter from another? Although Bryant definitely had more than just a splinter in his eye, she wouldn't do him much help if she was sick herself.

"That I am, got my bag and everything."

"How'd you get that?" he said, looking at the duffle she had over her shoulder.

"Dani brought it to me. Some patients aren't allowed personal belongings because they're a danger to themselves or others, but I'm allowed a relative amount of freedom."

"That's good then. That sundress you were wearing yesterday was nice."

"Was it?" She didn't know why, but her heart stuttered at that.

"Yeah, it was. May I?"

He held his hand out and she startled at it, uncertain and surprised. After a brief struggle in her head, she slid her own hand into his.

"Oh," he muttered quietly. "I was just asking you for your bag."

Keiko felt herself blush outright and her eyes go wide. "Right. That makes sense."

"But... this is all right." He turned and offered his other hand, a bemused smile on his face.

This time Keiko knew what was going on, and she handed him the strap to her duffle. He took it easily, and they walked out together.

She was perfectly ready to make the trek to the parking garage, but she saw his car was right there and waiting for her.

"Oh, did you just get here?"

"I was actually getting coffee over at the café across the street when you texted me, it was perfect timing."

"That worked out then."

"Yeah, our luck has been turning around lately."

"I'm not so sure it's luck."

"Then what?" he asked, opening the door for her.

She shrugged. "Maybe God. Maybe it's all just coincidence."

"Well, I know which one of the two you believe," he said as she slipped into the car.

She chuckled, pulling her legs in so that he could close the door then go around the front of the car. Unlike all of the other Millers, he didn't own a massive truck. Instead it was some sort of speedy, expensive thing, the cost of which could probably feed a family of five for a year.

They hit the road without any other incident, the radio playing low while they zoomed along. She noticed he took the backroad way to do it, and she couldn't help but wonder if it was to spend more time with her.

No, that was self-absorbed to think. Maybe he was just worried about driving too fast with her in the car. That was silly, but flattering, nonetheless.

For once, their conversation wasn't about wounds or what was wrong with each other or the world. They talked about the countryside, the view, the forecast for the week, and all the emails they both no doubt had to catch up on.

She hadn't told the church exactly what was going on with her because some of the parishioners were too old or too set in their ways to understand. She'd heard far too many comments about how mental illnesses were made up or how depression was just in people's heads. She didn't want to lose any of her ministries by what essentially would be a lot of hurtful gossip.

But she did have to explain her sudden absence, so her excuse was that she had an emergency trip come up with one of her cousins who lived the state over. It was a flimsy excuse, but the only reason it worked was because her parents were off visiting some other relatives back in Hawaii.

Her parents being out of town was one of the reasons that she had been so alone, but it was certainly working out for her at the moment. It was that old hindsight, she supposed.

The hour and fifteen minutes the backroads took to get to

her place went too fast, and the next thing she knew he was pulling up next to her car.

"I'll take your bag in for you."

"Thanks."

There was something strange between them as they walked up the stairs. Like a sort of heaviness that weighed down the air, making it thick and cottony in her lungs. A balloon about to pop, almost, but when they entered her apartment, that tension dissipated instead of any sort of climactic conclusion.

She was just so glad to be home.

"Uh, I hope you don't mind. I came by and tidied up."

"You mean got rid of all of the evidence of my mental break?"

"Something along those lines."

She smiled at him and settled onto her couch. "I think I'll take a nap soon. I haven't been in my own bed in what feels like ages."

"That sounds like a good idea. Do you want me to make you some tea?"

"Yeah, that would be lovely."

"You want some chamomile?"

"I'll take the lavender-mint, please."

"All right. Any special directions?"

"Just put about a spoonful of leaves into my diffuser then boil water in my electric kettle. I'm sure you can figure out the rest."

"Sounds good. You just sit and let someone else take care of you for once."

She huffed as best she could. "I just spent about four days being completely taken care of by other people."

"I think that was more you just taking care of yourself. Sure, they were all there to be tools for you, but if you weren't leading the way, it wouldn't have been much help at all, would it?"

"When did you get so insightful?"

"I always have been," he said with a chuckle. "I just wasn't using my powers for good before. I'm trying to change that."

She didn't have a response, her body flushing from head to toe, so she just nodded faintly.

He was trying to change? Dr. Hyleir's words played through her head again.

More food for thought.

There was such a thing as too big of a meal, however, and she felt overfull of new information. Although she had been praying her head off at the clinic, it would most definitely do her a lot of good to go to a Bible study at the church. Get some support and affirmation from her friends there. The Bible had whole passages about Christians being sharpening stones and family to each other. She could definitely use some sharpening.

Sighing, she thought of all she would have to do to get to Bible study. Either she would need to get dressed, go in her car and drive to where it was just out of town, or she would have to walk. She didn't think she had that in her. Maybe next week, and she could just make sure she caught the sermon on Sunday.

"I didn't think I took that long on the tea," Bryant said, coming in and handing her a steaming mug.

"You didn't. No, I am incredibly grateful. I just was thinking about if I would get to Bible study tomorrow, but I don't think I have the wherewithal to get there. Silly, but the thought of driving or walking that far right now seems too exhausting."

"I can drive you."

She paused in mid-drink. "Pardon?"

"I don't mind driving you, sticking around, then busing you back home. Who knows, maybe I'll learn something."

Keiko set her drink down, almost wondering if he was messing with her. "Are you sure? You would be willing to do that?"

He gave her a wan smile. "It's the least I can do."

"I thought we already talked about that."

"We did, but it's still sinking in I guess."

"Mmmhmm, I'm sure." She took a sip of her tea. "Thank you. For everything."

"No problem. I'm happy to."

19

Keiko

"I'm not entirely sure that I won't burst into flames just by being here," Bryant said, eyeing the church nervously as they walked up the old steps.

"Believe it or not, immolation isn't really the Lord's thing."

"Yeah, it's not the Lord in me that I'm worried about combusting the moment that I step foot on holy ground."

"Are you telling me that you believe in Satan?"

"I'm not sure what I believe at this point."

Interesting.

"Don't worry. I'll put the fire out if you do burst into flames. I really do appreciate you coming here with me."

"Of course. It's not that big a deal."

"Yes, it is. I want you to know that this is a very big deal to both you and me."

There was the slightest bit of coloring to his high cheekbones. He tilted his head downward, giving her that same look through his lashes, which made her knees feel... less than robust.

"Shucks, you don't have to butter me up. I'm already here."

She just rolled her eyes and headed inside, Bryant right behind her. His normal swagger was diminished; she could hear it in his steps.

She was proud of him though, probably far more proud than she had any right to be. She knew the Church was probably the second-to-last place he wanted to be next to his family's place.

And yet he was there. For *her*.

It was hard not to let that go to her head.

But she didn't. She just calmly walked to their Bible study room and found a seat.

They were early, of course.

She figured it would be easier for them to already be in the room and settled rather than making an entrance with all eyes on them. Bryant sat next to her, and she reached into her purse to hand him one of her spare Bibles.

"You think of everything, don't you?" he asked with a chuckle.

"It's a Bible study. I thought it might help if you were equipped."

"Good thinking."

"I do try."

"So what are we studying today?"

"I'm not sure. I'm not leading this one so it'll be up to whoever prepared the lesson."

"Oh, so it's not a chronological order thing? I'm not gonna be lost by coming in during the sequel?"

She chuckled a moment before joshing him with her arm. "Shhh, behave yourself."

"I'm trying. It's just so *boring*."

"Hey, you're the one who offered to come."

"I know, I know. I'm a real martyr."

She was sure the banter would have continued, but more people started to come in and Bryant clammed up. Keiko didn't miss the double takes that several people took, but she internally praised the Lord that no one said anything. She was absolutely sure that he wouldn't have taken it well.

So instead, they all settled in and started to go over Peter and how he denied Jesus three times.

...that was uncanny.

She almost wondered if Cameron, the man who ran the Bible study for her while she was gone, had done it on purpose. But there was no way that he could have known.

They sat there talking about someone denying the Lord and forgiveness and all sorts of things that probably hit close to home.

But Bryant made it to the end of the lesson, and when she glanced over to him, his expression was patient and... maybe a bit guilty. He didn't stand until everyone else did, but when people started to converse and socialize, he gently gripped her arm.

"Hey, where's the bathroom?"

She could tell by the look in his eyes that he didn't need the facilities for any practical reason, so she gave him what she hoped was an understanding smile. "We can go now, if you want."

"No, no. I just need a few minutes to myself. Stay here, uh, build each other up and all that."

"You know about that?"

"I told you, eighteen years of church, at least a few things stuck."

"Well, I'm glad that was one of the things that did."

She quickly gave him the directions to the closest set of bathrooms, and he rushed off, leaving her with her friends and fellow parishioners.

"Hey there, Keiko! Good to see you again," Milly said, hurrying up to her. Milly was a nice girl, about nineteen years old and quite the prodigious Bible-quizzer, but sometimes she could be too much for Keiko. "I can't remember the last time you've ever taken a break. It was like... three years ago, right?"

"Yeah, I got pneumonia during the winter."

"That was pretty bad, I remember. Ten different people in the congregation got it, right?"

"Almost twelve, actually. It was a pretty big epidemic."

"Yeah, thank goodness we didn't lose anyone. You're a real asset to this church, you know that? There are a lot of people who look to you for guidance."

Keiko's stomach flipped at that. "Well, I, uh, don't know if that's entirely true. I just do what I can."

The young woman reached out and gently stroked Keiko's arms. "You do so much more than that. Don't kneecap your accomplishments."

"I'll try not to."

"Good!" She beamed broadly. "By the way, I have a birthday party next month and I'd love to have you come! I'll send you an e-vite!"

"Yes, you do that."

Thankfully, Samson—her boyfriend—came up alongside her and snagged her, saying something about them being late. Keiko doubted they actually were, but the two had been together since sophomore year and he'd learned plenty of ways to handle her.

There were a few more minutes of hanging around and talking until Keiko was teetering towards exhaustion. She excused herself, then headed towards the bathroom.

Just as she expected, Bryant was there, fiddling with his phone as he leaned against the wall.

He made a striking picture, that was for certain. His hair was slightly curling and thick, cut shorter than most of his brothers. The sunlight was streaming in from the closest window, spilling across one side of his face and highlighting the strong bones that ran so commonly in the Miller family line.

"Hey there," he said softly, pushing off the wall.

"Hey," she said, holding her hand out to him. "Are you ready to go?"

"Are you?"

"Yeah. I'm getting pretty worn down."

"Then all right, let's head out."

"Yeah, we can do that." She realized that once again she wasn't quite ready to go home. "But maybe I could use something to eat."

"Really? You want to go to the diner?"

That seemed like a good idea for a moment, but then she shook her head. "Too many people, and I don't think I have it in me for a sit-down place."

"There's not really any fast food around here though."

"No, there isn't," she said slowly. "... but there is in the city."

"Why, Ms. Keiko Albryte, are you asking me to take you on a jaunt to the city?"

"I just might be. Maybe if you're game for it."

"Aren't you too tired?"

"I'm too tired for social stuff or driving myself, but I think I could stand a couple of hours in the car with you."

"If I didn't know better, I would say you were complimenting me."

"Yeah, yeah, don't get a big head."

They walked out the doors together, hand in hand, and Keiko couldn't help but wonder if it was a new future that they were walking into.

"Is it offensive if I say I'm surprised you eat fast food?" Bryant asked as they drove back to her apartment after having a delicious Mexican meal.

"It's usually not a great idea to bring up my eating disorder all the time. Makes it seem like I can't escape it or it's what defines me. But I understand with everything we've been through that you might have a few questions."

"Oh, okay, so don't ask questions unless they're urgent or we're already talking about that, got it."

"Funny, you say that like you think we'll be hanging out often."

"Would that be such a bad thing?"

Like a teenage girl, Keiko felt an exciting sort of fizziness fill her up. "No, no, it wouldn't."

"Good to know."

"I'm glad you think so."

"Yeah, yeah I do."

That fizziness turned to warmth, and she sank deeper into her seat. She was beginning to feel things that she never really had before, warm and effervescent and bubbly. It made her nervous, but it also thrilled her in a way she didn't expect.

Once more, they got to her apartment way too fast, and she looked at her front door, not wanting the car ride to be over yet. She'd been enjoying the conversation so much.

"Let me walk you to your door," Bryant said, parking and getting out to help her.

"You really don't have to," she said as he opened her door.

"I know I don't have to, but I want to."

All right. How could she argue with that?

She let him escort her up the steps and hold her leftover food container from the restaurant while she unlocked the door. She thought about inviting him in, about making tea and chit-chatting, but she did feel exhaustion starting to bite in at the corners of her mind. Considering how newly recovered she was, she needed to take it easy and sleep.

Besides, she wouldn't mind a nice one-on-one with God to go over everything she'd observed from the Bible study session.

"Thank you again for the ride."

"Ah, don't worry about it." He licked his lips.

She realized that they were awfully close to each other, standing face to face in her doorway. She was acutely aware of everything about his body, the heat emanating from him and the deep, assured cadence of his breathing. It wouldn't take much movement at all to bring the two of them together. And then...

And then what?

She'd been so busy with her life and her purpose that she'd never even kissed anyone. Twenty-six years old and as inexperienced as they came. And one didn't go from having no attraction to anyone for all that time to suddenly wanting to kiss the prodigal son of a family her life had inexplicably gotten wrapped up with. That wasn't how it worked!

...was it?

Who knew? She'd have to talk to Dr. Hyleir about it when she saw her next week.

"Do you need a ride to church on Sunday, too?"

She blinked at him, taken off guard. "Really? You'd take me to Sunday School and the sermon?"

"Sure, why not? I didn't burst into flames the first time, so I'm pretty sure I won't spontaneously combust."

"All right then. Yeah, I'd love that."

"Cool. What time should I show up?"

"I usually head out at seven-thirty."

"Seven-thirty!?"

He let out a laugh. Instead of watching his face, her eyes went to the movement of his chest. And how muscular it looked through his shirt.

"You do know what the word weekend means, right?" he said.

"I've got a fair enough idea. You don't have to if you don't want to."

"No, no. It's fine. I want to. I'll see you this Sunday, bright and early."

"It's a plan."

He tipped his head in a nod that brought their faces so close together that she hardly dared to breathe. He paused a moment, as if he was going to tilt his face down and close the distance between them, but he didn't. Instead, he pulled back and headed out the door.

Huh. That was certainly something else.

20

Bryant

Since he'd seen Keiko at what was probably her worse, he'd been trying to train himself not to use terms like psycho or mental. Now that he knew how hard it was to have a mental illness, and how even the strongest, most put-together person could struggle with their own brain betraying them, those terms seemed rude. Mean.

But still, even with trying to change his way of thinking, he couldn't help but wonder if he was crazy for going to a Sunday sermon.

His only comfort was that they were going to the earlier one, which wasn't the one his family favored. Unlike Keiko, they liked to sleep in and would go to the service that was held at eleven.

Also, unlike Keiko, they didn't set up the breakfast, put out all the coffee things, and make sure the whole building was ready to go by the time its doors opened at eight a.m. sharp. Because apparently Keiko and two older ladies were the hands and brains who ran the operation.

Bryant would have thought it was the Pastor and his wife who at least had somewhat of a hand in things, but nope, it was just the trio of women. Of course, since he had suddenly become Keiko's shadow, the two older ladies were more than happy to order him around in a way that was frankly quite adorable.

So, after making sure there were bags in just about every trashcan in the place, unlocking all the doors, and reaching higher shelves to water the plants that were in some of the rooms, he almost felt like he was useful.

Which was a strange thing for him to be feeling in a church.

But as nice as that feeling was, it didn't soothe the growing unease in him as they approached the time where people would start showing up. Although his family *probably* wouldn't be there so early, there would definitely be plenty of people who recognized him. And those people who recognized him were sure to go and tell his family all about how their black sheep of the family was in church trying to get his wool white again.

Which he wasn't. He just wanted to help Keiko. And if one thing was certain, the church definitely helped Keiko.

Something had changed between them since he had found her in that terrible state. He didn't have a word for it, and it wasn't like anything he had felt before, but it was *there.*

He told her things he never told anyone before. Secrets and old, shameful memories. She knew all of the worst parts of him, both from his own mouth and his family's, but she didn't seem to care.

Which she should have. If anyone should care, it was her.

She was the holy and perfect church girl who helped people and barely ever thought about herself.

And yet she seemed to want to spend time with him. She suggested a two-hour drive to the city just to grab cheap burritos and chips with him. She listened when he talked, and she never told him he was stupid or crazy for any of the things that he said.

She didn't give in to him all the time either. She called him out when he said something not so great, and she challenged him when it was appropriate too. It was completely different from all the yes-men he had with his empire.

And speaking of his empire, he'd pretty much handed it over for his board to run for the past week. He'd never done it before, mostly because he was sure that none of them could run it as well as he could. He was the business genius after all and the charming face of the company.

But so far, they were doing a pretty good job.

Maybe he didn't have to be at the helm of everything every day. There could be other things to life besides accruing more wealth, boozing, and partying.

Maybe.

But he would have to survive the whole church thing first.

Of course, Keiko couldn't just tuck herself away while everyone socialized. She had to be in the thick of it, checking on coffee, putting out more cream cheese. And *boy*, could some people go through cream cheese.

So, Bryant tucked himself between some tall plants and tried to cling to the shadows as best he could. It seemed to work, because the only people who noticed him were a couple of little kids who were running around.

Thankfully, the kids didn't have any idea who he was, and they dismissed him as another adult they wanted nothing to do with. Perhaps it was ironic, but by some miracle, he made it to the sermon without being discovered. He knew that once they were all seated together and in the same room, there would be no hiding, but at least he could postpone it as long as possible.

"You ready?" she asked when everyone had begun to file into the main room.

"As ready as I'll ever be," he answered, following along behind her.

"We can sit towards the back. I don't volunteer for things during the sermon so I can fully experience it and not worry about tasks."

"Yeah, heaven forbid you miss a verse on a hymn."

"Yes, that's definitely the reason. A complete fear of messing up a religious song."

"Sounds about right."

"*Shhh*, it's starting."

She joshed his arm again, her elbow pressing into him, and he quieted. But where she had touched him grew warm, like it was licked by fire. It certainly made it hard to concentrate, but he put on his most neutral face and listened.

The sermon actually wasn't that bad. It was centered around love, and the three different words the Greeks had for it. The message bit at his pride, but it was pretty fascinating for what it was.

Fascinating, but not quite worth getting up at six-thirty a.m. to get dressed.

Toward the end of it, when things were winding down, he fought the urge to twiddle his thumbs. But Keiko seemed completely into it, leaning forward in her seat, the slender column of her neck extended. Her dark eyes were focused forward, her brows furrowed ever so slightly.

She made quite the picture, and he wished that he could

document it forever. It was such a still moment of quiet intensity, something that felt precious but also private at the same time.

The pastor said something that he didn't catch, and then she was standing. He must have jerked to attention, startled, because she looked back to him with a smile.

She whispered, "It's all right. Stay here. There's just something I have to do."

"Oh... okay."

He wracked his brain as he tried to remember what part of the service they were in, but it wasn't until she was halfway down the aisle to kneel at the altar that he remembered.

Right, it was a call to prayer. Everyone was free to stay in their seat with their heads bowed, but those who felt they needed some extra support and fellowship could go down to the front.

The whole things seemed embarrassing and put-on-the-spot in his opinion, but from what he could see from Keiko's face, she looked relieved more than anything else.

In fact, he couldn't take his eyes off her.

He watched as she knelt, going from somewhere around five-eight to so much smaller, curled as she was on the cushioned bench. She looked tiny, almost childlike, and completely alone.

Worry bubbled up within him. Concern. He didn't like how it looked, her completely by herself, but before he could figure out what to do or if he should do anything at all, an older woman stood up and hobbled her way towards Keiko. Assured and comforting, she laid her hand on the young woman's shoulder and began to pray too.

Almost as soon as she was there, a younger woman stood up and joined them. Then an older man. Then a couple of people that he was pretty sure he had seen at the wedding. Within just moments, there was a crowd around her, all praying, some of them with their hands lifted to heaven, some saying things under their breath.

It was... *beautiful*, and in that moment, he got it.

He finally, really got it.

There was a connection between all of them. Vibrant and warm and strong. Burning with something untouchable, and yet they were all shrouded in it.

They were all strengthened by it, fueled by it, made stronger. It gave them something to be besides themselves, something greater than just them. They had purpose. They had community.

There really was more to life than partying and getting high and chasing that next rush.

And these people had found it. There was value in building relationships and community.

He sat there, utterly shocked by the revelation he was experiencing. It felt like it was scrubbing out old connections and rules that his mind had made and rebuilding new ones, making theories and asking questions he never thought to ask.

He wasn't sure what all of it meant, his brain didn't feel nearly powerful enough to compute all of that out, but all he knew was that he had several different paths in front of him, all wound around her and what they could possibly mean to each other.

But if he moved forward, he was probably going to have to leave the path he was on behind. The one he was comfortable with and knew oh so well.

But he was pretty sure she was worth it.

21

Keiko

*L*ife got better in little increments, so subtle that they were basically unnoticeable at first. But once she started looking back, she realized how far she had come since her most recent low.

She felt less like she was teetering on the brink, her feet growing more and more secure under her every day. And while she didn't get to see Dani as much, considering her best friend was a newlywed and she and Benji were building a cabin for themselves between the two ranches, she did manage to sync up her schedule with Sophia again.

And despite the fact that Sophia was probably one of the people who had been most inconvenienced by Keiko's breakdown, she never said anything. In fact, she almost seemed more comfortable during their meals and rides.

Or maybe that was Bradley's influence, helping Sophia discover herself and move through her recovery.

If Keiko was being honest with herself, she would have to admit that Bryant was helping her too.

In fact, he was helping a whole lot.

She had never expected him to bring her meals regularly, or go grocery shopping with her, but he did. And while their worlds didn't revolve around each other—he still had his business and she had her friends, work, and the church—they did spend quite a lot of time together.

He started coming to church with her. Not always, and not even every week, but enough that people started to murmur and recognize it. Several times when she visited his family for various reasons, someone would bring him up, but she would always tell them that it was up to him if he initiated contact or not.

But she had hope that he would. And the more time that they spent together, the more she felt like that was a possibility.

And the more she began to *feel*.

It began as small, sparky things that reminded her of the first thunderstorm of summer or a sparkler after it got dark. Then it grew into something deeper. Something more refined and filling.

Sure, it was still nerve-wracking, that was for certain, but it was a good kind of uncertainty.

Or at least mostly good.

She still was nervous on occasion, or felt pushed into things she wasn't ready for, overwhelming things, but she tried not to pay the anxiety too much mind. For the moment, she didn't see a reason why she couldn't let herself *feel*.

And she felt a lot, like when Bryant would come over and let her pitch her next Bible study premise to him, or a review that she had written for the slideshow at the library she worked at. Sometimes he came over to just have tea and chat.

She'd never thought she'd ever be alone with an unmarried man in her own place, but he always kept a respectful distance. And while he still flirted plenty, he never tried to cross a line like he had when he was shirtless in her living room.

So naturally, when her phone rang a month after their first church service together, she still felt a thrill of excitement when his name popped up.

"Hey there, what are you up to?"

"You know that it's my one day without the library or church duties," she answered, laughing as she stirred her tea. It was a lemon and basil combination this time, one of her newer and more herbal recipes.

"That's right, I guess I do have a pretty good handle on your schedule. But still, I wanted to be polite and ask if I could take you somewhere."

Despite all the progress that they had made, her mind instantly flashed to the Bistro. "Um... that's really nice, but I don't think I'm mentally ready to go on any sort of date right now. Even a simple one—"

"Whoa, hold on. Who said anything about a date? There's just something that I want to take you to as a friend. I think it could help you, and I promise there's absolutely zero romance at all."

"Really?" she asked suspiciously, raising her eyebrow even though he couldn't see her. "Zero romance at all?"

"Yup. Zero. A grand sum of nada."

"All right. I suppose you've earned my trust enough for that."

"Aw, you flatter me so."

She chuckled, rolling her eyes. "So what time should I be ready by?"

"Give me about two hours. Wear something comfortable."

"Oh, are you taking me to the paintball field again?"

"As much as I am sure you'd love showing all of us up again, no, it's not that. You'll never guess it, not in a million years."

"A million years is a long time."

"And still you're not gonna guess it."

She laughed, and they finished up the conversation. When they hung up, she felt a thrill of excitement, which really didn't make sense.

She had meant what she said when she had told Bryant that she wasn't ready to date. Because she wasn't. She was still trying to figure out if what she felt was attraction or a crush or anything of that nature. It felt silly to be wondering about such things that most people dealt with during their teenage years, but she had always done things at her own pace.

And yet, despite that trepidation, she was still filled with anticipation. She looked forward to seeing him and the fizzy warmth that filled her belly whenever he flashed that grin at her.

She spent far too much time figuring out what she wanted to wear, and only a buzz from her phone managed to get her out of her room and rushing towards her door to put on her shoes.

In the doorway she paused, her hands itching and wanting to pat each corner of the entry to make sure everything was safe. It was a new ritual that had manifested since her break-down, which Dr. Hyleir warned her might happen.

It was frustrating to feel like she was doing better just to have reminders shoehorn themselves into her face that she was sick, and it was a chronic illness that would never be *gone*. But thankfully, she was distracted from the compulsion by a strong knock from below.

She looked down the stairs and could see Bryant standing outside the door, his upper half visible in the pretty little window. Just like he'd told her to be, he was dressed in casual clothes, a pair of nice jeans and a soft-looking sweatshirt. His hair was slicked back, and he looked both fresh and excited.

"You ready to go?" he asked, shooting her a smile once she came down the stairs.

"That's why I came down here."

"Hah, good. I left the car running. Let's go."

For perhaps the dozenth time, she slipped into his car and they headed for the city. They'd made the trip so often that it was basically a ritual at that point, and she settled in.

The conversation flowed much easier than it once had, with him asking about her upcoming plans and her asking if he'd had any stories about ridiculous clients and their impossible expectations. It was a give and take, and she let herself relax.

However, that sense of relaxation faded as they pulled up to a building tucked away on a busy city block that she didn't recognize at all. It was clean, and there was a single business sign with the word "SMASH," but that was the only indication of what it could possibly be.

"Is this a comic thing?" Keiko asked, thinking back to the times he'd told her about how he would hide under his sheets with a flashlight to read about various superheroes when he was a pre-teen.

Bryant laughed as he moved around to open her door. "Not really, but I see how you made the association."

"All right, then where are we then?"

"Let's just say that this is something that might help you turn the other cheek."

"I didn't know I had an issue with that."

"Isn't that just human nature by this point?"

"Okay, that might be true."

She dropped her guard and decided to just trust him. That was the whole reason she'd even come, wasn't it?

But she still wasn't any closer to understanding where she was even when they *did* go inside, and Bryant paid for an hour package. They also had to sign some sort of legal waver as well and wasn't *that* interesting.

They were led to a "changing room," and the employee handed them both white jumpsuits that reminded her of what painters wore as well as covers for their shoes.

"What on earth could we possibly need these for?" she asked as they were led down a long hall and to another room.

"You'll see," was all he said, and she felt like he was enjoying the suspense way more than he should have.

Eventually, however, they were finally stopped in front of a door and the employee unlocked it for them. "Your timer starts the moment I close this. Please remember to have fun, don't hurt yourselves, and smash away!"

"Smash away?"

Keiko had questions, that was for certain, but then they were walking forward and into a stark white room with a table with various items on it in the center and... an entire old car?

"What is this place?" she asked, so thoroughly confused.

"This, my friend, is a smash room. Our tools are on the table, and we have an hour to mess up this room however we want.

"You wanna smash all the windows? Then smash the hood? You wanna throw this neon paint all over the white walls? We can do that too. It's just pure, wanton destruction, with the bonus of everything being recycled once it's damaged beyond repair."

Keiko stared at the mass of things. She saw a TV box, a microwave, several cardboard boxes, a tea set on a glass table, just plenty of fragile and shatterable things.

"Why would I want to break these things?" she asked cautiously.

"There's a whole bunch of reasons. One, a lot of times we have to hold our temper in, even when really terrible, unfair things happen. People who don't deserve promotions get them, killers get away with murder, and abusers get made into the victim. People lie and cheat and end up successful instead of punished." Bryant walked around looking at items.

He continued, "Plus, there's the control aspect."

"Control?"

"Yeah, from what you've told me with your OCD, it's kinda like your brain is forcing you to think and feel certain things rather than you actively deciding them. With this, you're in charge of everything.

"Besides..." He picked up a plate and chucked it at the wall, resulting in it exploding into a bunch of ceramic pieces that fell to the covered floor with a pleasant little tinkle. "It's kind of a fascinating study of how certain objects interact."

Keiko remembered when she had once put an egg in the microwave just to see what it would do. That was the thing about childhood; there was so much curiosity, so much to learn and observe.

"I suppose I have always wanted to know how much force it would take to shatter an old TV box." She'd seen it so many times in action and spy movies that she remembered it definitely being a question she asked herself. Especially since the sparks were always so impressive.

"That's my girl. Now let's get to smashing."

Although he emboldened her by throwing another plate, Bryant let her take the lead. She decided what tools they used on what, starting off small and building up higher and higher until she was taking a sledgehammer to the front of the old car.

She wasn't normally one who took much comfort in destruction. She liked to create and maintain order and just generally make things better. But there was something *fun* about letting go and doing whatever she wanted to a whole bunch of very breakable things.

For example, she held the teapot high above her head and thought about when she was younger, and everyone in her class but her and Dani got invited to Rachel's birthday slumber party. She put all of that pain, all of that humiliation into the cheap porcelain then threw it right onto the ground.

And just like that, it felt like the pain was dealt with. Absolved.

Bryant was right. It really was an exercise in catharsis. She splashed red paint all over the walls when she thought about how angry her OCD made her sometimes with losing time and expending energy. She splashed orange when she thought of all those years she wasted hating her body and wishing she could just be thin enough to maybe be beautiful.

She threw a brick through the microwave when she thought about how the girls used to gang up on Dani and how a couple of guys would ask her out as jokes. She flipped over the glass table when she thought about children that didn't have enough food to eat, or how money had become so much more valuable than human life.

She screamed, she shouted, she laughed, and she cheered giddily. Endorphins rushed through her and for a time in the smash room, she really did feel joyous and free.

By the time the hour ended, she was covered in sweat under her suit and utterly exhausted. All of her limbs felt like jelly. She wobbled as they walked out and returned their suits to a bin that was labeled for it in the hall and then discarded their shoe covers.

"So, what do you think?" Bryant asked, looking much less breathless than her when they reached the parking lot but still had a ruddy-cheeked face.

"I feel like I should probably be worried about how good that was for me, but that was like, *really* good."

"Don't worry about it. I figured you spend so much of your life trying to manage something that's pretty stressful while also helping everyone else around you, it would be nice to cut loose and throw a real temper tantrum." He looked at her out of the corner of his eye. "You do know what a temper tantrum is, right, Saint Keiko?"

She playfully joshed his shoulder, although her arm was so tired that it took more effort than she would like to admit. "Just because I'm not an expert like you doesn't mean that I've never been a little naughty myself."

He made a choking sound at that, which was more than a little bit amusing. "Uh, I think you and I have very different definitions of what the word naughty should be used for."

"Yeah, I'm sure we do." It was borderline flirting, and she knew that, but it didn't make her fearful. No, it just made her feel... safe?

That didn't make much sense.

But maybe it didn't need to. Maybe she could just be in the moment with Bryant and enjoy coming down from her adrenaline.

Turning to him, she took in all the detail of his face. The strong lines, the grin, the way his dark hair would sometimes shine red in the direct sunlight. He was handsome, that much had never changed, but there was something more to him now. Something familiar and welcoming.

"Thank you," she said, a feeling building in her chest again. "Like really, really thank you."

He looked at her, and the way he tilted his head made her heart pound ridiculously hard. That feeling, strange and alien, burst into bloom as the next words left his mouth.

"Anything for you."

22

Bryant

*B*ryant's life had changed so much in the past three months, so thoroughly that it was almost unrecognizable.

It hadn't really started as something intentional. Really, his whole goal at first was to just be there for Keiko and repay the kindness that she had shown him. But then he had started attending church more and helping her with her various ministries, and he figured if he wanted to be useful, he needed to know more of what she was talking about.

So he started reading the Bible. Mostly all the parts with Jesus because those were the ones Keiko liked to focus on the most. After a solid month and a half of helping her, he was pretty sure he was able to figure out why.

It was because Jesus' teachings were all about love and forgiveness. About cherishing your fellow man and your neighbor and the evils of riches. The son of God himself hung out with tax collectors and prostitutes, not judging them, but guiding them by letting them know they were loved, they were valued. That they were worth good things.

He could see how that would bring comfort to her. Being one of maybe three Asians in a small town, and a person who struggled with mental health, couldn't have been easy. It obviously still wasn't easy. And so, he studied and studied, and eventually those words started to sink in.

He turned over more of his business to his board, letting them take over duties that he had been so controlling over before. And while he didn't agree with some Christian's thoughts that gambling was inherently evil, he did make some major changes to his business.

First of all, he invited a gambling addiction expert to come and do a weeklong training session with his employees that taught them how to spot signs of people struggling with a spiral and what to do to help them. He had signs put up that were apparently supposed to help with that as well and hired two on-site counselors. He established time limits, and even funded a support group. Was it perfect? No, but he felt it was a good start.

As for his alcohol, they were changing their marketing strategy and adding lines about drinking responsibly. He also had his R&D department working on a non-alcoholic drink for designated drivers and sober folks who still wanted to have fun and enjoy parties without just holding a glass of water. That was going to take a long while, but he was glad to at least have gotten started.

As for himself, he still enjoyed the bottle from time to time, but it was just that: something to be enjoyed. Not a crutch to live with himself or be able to look in the mirror. He was still debating quitting it all together because it wasn't adding anything to his life, but he figured going slow and taking manageable steps was better for him than trying to revolutionize his life overnight.

How strange to think that all of these changes were because of Keiko. She had told him that it was wrong of her to try to "fix" him, and yet he felt like he was being slowly repaired over time. Like all the little cracks in him, where the bitterness and distrust seeped out, were being slowly filled in by her kindness, her wisdom, really, everything about her.

She made him want to be a better person in a way he never had before. She made him look outside of himself and at the greater world. Instead of always thinking about his next thrill, he would instead think about the next thing he could create, or a new idea to nurture. It was more fulfilling to him than any of the parties or women, and he wondered how he had lived when he had been so clearly starving for so long.

But with all that progress, with all the happiness that bloomed in his chest whenever he looked at her, there was still something that he had to do before he could *really* move forward.

He was terrified of it, though.

But he *had* to.

He could feel that something was building up between him and Keiko. Something tentative. Fragile, like a tiny baby bird. They trusted each other, they confided in each other, but there was still a caution to their interactions.

He knew that she wasn't ready to date, and he also knew that he wasn't remotely worthy of dating her. But maybe, if he dealt with that one thing, he could become the kind of man who could be good enough for her.

Because he wanted desperately to be good enough for her. Especially when she would look at him in those quiet moments, a sweet smile on her full lips and the slightest bit of pink on her cheekbones. He could see so much behind her eyes, she *trusted* him with seeing that, and that made him feel more accepted than anything else that he could remember.

So, in the hopes that it would help him grow, he knew that he needed to talk to his family.

Really talk.

The thought made him nauseous. There were so many years of hurt. Mud thrown on both sides and wounds that were too deep to ignore. It would be a messy talk. Uncomfortable.

But the longer he procrastinated, the longer that caution stayed between them. At least he knew he didn't have to do it alone.

If there was anything Keiko had made clear, it was that he didn't have to be alone for anything anymore if he didn't want to.

Strangely enough, it was a Thursday when he suddenly found the courage to call her. Like usual, she picked up on the first ring, sounding surprised but happy to hear him.

"Hey there, friend," she said, and he could just picture the smile on her face as she did.

"Hey. Are you free this afternoon?"

"I was supposed to go shoe shopping with Chastity now that her feet have gone down from all that pregnancy swelling, but she canceled because the little one might have a cold."

"Oh gee, that doesn't sound fun."

"No, it doesn't. I'm not exactly the biggest fan of very young babies, anyway, so I'll admit I'm guiltily relieved."

Bryant was about to ask why but then he thought of how babies liked to spit-up, pee, and poop at random times and how that might be difficult for Keiko to deal with on a bad day.

"Ugh, that sucks for her, but I'll be greedy and say it works out for me." He also made a mental note to buy a very belated baby gift for Chastity. He hadn't realized he'd missed such an important event.

Probably because he wasn't invited to any baby showers or included in family announcement letters.

That just reiterated his need to fix things, so he cleared his throat. "I was wondering if you would... if you would help me talk to my family."

The line was quiet for a moment, and he almost thought they were disconnected.

"Really? Today?"

"Yeah, I'm not saying it'll be solved today, but today is when we make the first attempt."

He didn't miss the excitement that crept into her tone, and it gave him hope.

"Yeah, of course. I can be ready in ten minutes."

He chuckled at that, her enthusiasm making him feel far braver than he was. "I'll need at least an hour and a half to get to you, so don't worry."

"Oh, okay. I'll take a shower then."

"Sounds like a plan. I'll see you soon."

"See you soon."

He was about to hang up when he heard her call his name. "Yes?"

"I'm really proud of you."

She hung up after that, but Bryant stood there in his penthouse, holding his phone. He would probably never admit it, but those five little words meant so much more than Keiko could ever know.

~

BRYANT LOOKED up the steps that lead to the porch of his family's main house. It almost looked like a scene in a western. Ma was sitting in her rocking chair with Sophia curled in a chair beside her, dutifully sketching on her tablet; Pa was in the doorway, arms crossed and looking passive as usual, while Ben and Bart sat on the railing on the far side of the porch.

The only one who was missing was Bradley, which made Bryant's stomach twist, but then Bradley showed up with a bottle of water in his hand and actually walked down the step to stand next to him.

"Hey there, brother," he said, a small smile on his face.

"Hey, brother."

All right, this was it. He was looking at his family and they were looking at him, and suddenly there was a whole lot of feelings from a whole lot of years rising up to the surface very quickly.

Keiko must have sensed the rush because her hand slipped into his and she squeezed it gently. "You can do this," she said, her words just for him.

Hey, she hadn't been wrong yet.

"It's good to see you," Ma said, her expression soft but sad.

It made that familiar knife twist in Bryant's heart. But instead of getting defensive, he felt the emotion and then processed it. Like Keiko said all the time, discomfort was temporary and sometimes it just had to be weathered.

"It's good to see you too." He took a deep breath. He could do this. "Look, I know we haven't always seen eye to eye—"

"That's an understatement," Bart scoffed before Ma quickly hushed him.

"I came here because I wanted to talk. There's been this rift between us for too long, and I'm not naïve enough to think that we can fix it right here and now, but I was hoping it could start today.

"I know that I have been selfish and hurtful. I know I have said mean, hurtful things. I know I've made several of you uncomfortable. And I know that I chose a style of living that broke your hearts."

Surprisingly, this wasn't the hard part. He knew what he'd done was wrong, and he'd prepared his apology at least a hundred times in his head. And the more he spoke, the more an ease started to settle over him. It wasn't anything relaxing, per se, but it was a sort of peace with himself that he hadn't felt in years.

"So, I want all of you to know that I am sorry. Really, deeply and truly sorry. I want to be better. I want to be a son that you can be proud of. I know that will take time, and you don't have to accept my apology, but I would really, *really*, like to build a future where we're in each other's lives."

It was so quiet that Bryant was pretty sure they could have heard a pin drop. The only sounds were the standard ambient noises of the farm, and they faded to the back of his mind as he looked at each of his relatives in turn.

Of course, it was Ma who moved first. She stood, practically running to the steps, and threw open her arms.

"If someone told me today was the day I was getting my baby boy back, I would have worn something worthy of the occasion."

Bryant didn't have words for the emotions that flooded through him. Relief, acceptance, happiness, love, it was a complex and heady mix that made his head spin. But not so much that he couldn't rush up the stairs and envelop her in a hug.

It had been so many years since they had embraced, since

he had felt the warmth and comfort that only came from hugging a mother that he missed terribly, that they held it for a long, long time. In fact, it wasn't until Bradley cleared his throat that they parted.

"I'm really, really happy to hear that, but I would like to be the first person in the family to apologize to you. Because I do think we all owe you one."

"Owe him one?" Bart asked incredulously. "What did we even do?"

Bradley walked up the stairs, placing his hand on Bryant's shoulder. "I know we talked before, but I'm really sorry I wasn't there for you like a brother should have been. I'm sorry I failed you by letting you feel like you were alone and couldn't trust any of us. I should have stood up for you when our older brothers and schoolmates teased you for the things you like, especially since I always did it for my friends.

"I love you, brother, and I appreciate how smart you are, and all those crazy puzzles you liked to solve. I miss you, and I regret all the years we missed out together because I was too concerned with fitting in."

"Wait," Ben said, standing and crossing around to the front of the porch. "I don't understand. What do you mean you felt alone?"

This was the hard part that Bryant had been dreading. How to explain to his family that actions when he was young had started him on his path. He didn't want to sound petulant, or like an idiot. He didn't want to sound like he was condemning them. But he did need them to know that he hadn't just flown off the handle for no reason. They needed to know how he'd felt ostracized. Not good enough for the illustrious Miller name.

"When I was younger, none of you would accept my

hobbies or the things I liked to do. And when I did accomplish something that was important to me, you didn't care."

"What?" Bart asked, his tone rising. "Name one instance."

"Well, how about when Bryant made it to the Mathletics finals for our entire state and none of us attended it," Bradley said. "Or how we have a whole display cabinet downstairs for football, basketball and swimming trophies, but none of my awards from theater or Bryant's trophies from ICE or robotics. Not even any of those models that he loved have made it onto a display in the house."

Bart seemed to back down, clearly replaying memories in his head.

"I... I think I remember that."

But Bryant knew that he couldn't let Bradley fight his battle for him. "I know I was a weird kid, into comics and fantasy and all that, but I can't count how many times you guys called me a freak or weird. I remember you guys begging mom to not have to take me places because I was so annoying.

"And Ma, you remember that big blow out we had about the models?"

She nodded; her lips pressed into a thin line. But it didn't look aggressive, but almost... worried? Guilty? He couldn't quite say.

"I remember."

"I know that you were stressed and you were raising five young men pretty far apart in age, but I'll never forget how you took me aside, looked me in my eyes, and asked why I couldn't have been more like Ben."

"I... I thought that you were just being difficult on purpose."

"I wasn't," he answered, bolstered by her not calling him a liar or weak. "I mean, I know I *was*, but it wasn't on purpose. I don't know why I'm so different from the rest of you. I don't know why I don't like camping or roughhousing or being rough and tumble. I don't know why I like designer things and art and learning strange factoids that will never really be of use to anybody. But I am what I am, and I think I can bring things to this family that are of value."

There, he said it. Everything was out and in the open. They could reject him, tell him that he should get over it, but he had done what he needed to do.

But possibly the last thing he expected was for Ma to burst into tears and grab him again.

"Oh, my boy, my baby boy. I never even thought about it. I'm so, so sorry. You just always seemed like you wanted to be on your own."

"I was on my own to protect myself. I just wanted to be accepted."

"Please, please forgive me for ever making you ever feel like you weren't. I love you, sweetie, from your wizard cape to the dungeoneers and designers."

"That's not what it's called Ma but thank you. Thank you so much."

Bryant felt himself tear up, so he buried his head in her gray hair. He knew there was still a long road ahead of him, that there would be pitfalls and mistakes and things that came up later, but that was fine. The important thing was that they had at least started the journey.

The moment between them lasted for quite a while, so much so that he almost jolted when he felt a firm grip on his shoulder.

"Look, I'm sorry, brother," Bart said, pain written across his strong features. "I know now what it feels like to think you don't belong somewhere, so I'm sorry. I was young and stupid. I've learned a lot since then, you know."

"So have I," Bryant answered with a weak laugh, gripping his brother's hand in his.

That seemed to break the rest of the ice and his family closed in on him, hugging or extending a hand until they were all connected. It reminded him distinctly of that moment that Keiko had gone to the front of the church and had a whole chunk of the congregation pray over her.

The only one who didn't join in was Sophia, and judging by how she kept looking up and down from her tablet, tongue sticking slightly out of her mouth, Bryant would guess that she was drawing the moment in front of her. But that was fine with him because if he had his way, he would want to document it for all eternity.

Bryant Miller, the prodigal son, had finally returned home.

IT WAS A LONG, teary, and emotion-filled couple of hours spent talking and explaining and doing all the things that came along with repairing relationships that had been neglected for so long. When it was finally time to go, he was so utterly exhausted that he knew the journey back to the city was going to be borderline painful.

"Bryant?" Keiko's voice was small as she called his name, as if she was uncertain if she should speak. Personally, he loved the way she said anything, so if he had his way, she would talk all the time.

"Yeah?"

"May I ask you a question."

"I've never said no to that."

"I know. But it's personal."

"Fire away."

He heard her draw in an unsteady breath, and it made anticipation rise within him. Considering the afternoon that they had had together, what could she want to know?

"Why do you think you've changed so much recently?"

Ah.

He felt a smile slide across his features. Of course, she would want to know. He hadn't thought he was ready to say, but he had promised her honesty always, hadn't he?

"I realized that I want to be a better man. Someone who leaves behind a legacy to be proud of. You know, has made the world better when I hit that final curtain call.

"And I guess you can say that hanging around you made me realize that the things I thought were worthless and stupid were actually some of the most valuable things on this Earth."

He'd already taken one giant leap that day, why not another one?

So he continued, "Then, if I'm able to do all that, maybe one day I might be the kind of man who could deserve a woman like you."

Silence, utter silence filled his speedy little car and he felt his stomach drop. Keiko had told him she wasn't ready to date; why did he always have to push the line? She probably saw him as nothing more than a friend, and he needed to be grateful for that.

But then, so tentative he almost thought it was a stray hair brushing him, her hand reached out. Her fingers hovered over his hand, drawing his eyes partially from the road, before she finally settled it on top of his own.

"I think you're on the right track for that," she said with the kindest smile that had ever been turned in his direction. "I'm really glad that we're gonna be able to heal together."

"Yeah?" he asked, his throat squeezing so tight that he was surprised he could even speak.

"Yeah," she said, leaning over slightly and pressing a kiss to his cheek before returning to her seat.

Huh.

He had one heck of a future in store for him, didn't he?

23

Keiko

*S*ix months, two weeks and four days was all it took for Keiko's life to completely turn upside down in all the best ways possible.

Her mental health was at an all-time high, with her experiencing fewer rituals and fewer compulsions. She still went to Dr. Hyleir because it never hurt to be vigilant. She also had more support than ever, with Bryant becoming just as close with her as Dani, and the Millers becoming stronger and happier as a whole.

In fact, the only reason that she was feeling slightly down was because Bryant had been on a necessary business trip for the past week and, while they talked every night, it wasn't the same as his usual visits.

She didn't even want to think about how much money on gas he spent going between his place just on the other side of the city and hers, but it had to be a large number. Especially since he had taken to driving her to church every Sunday.

Even if he complained every Sunday about having to wake up so early.

Her phone rang and she answered it without looking. The only people who ever called her were Bryant and Dr. Hyleir, so she had taken to just accepting the call by default.

"Hey there," Bryant's voice came over the line, and even though they had just talked the night before, she still felt a flutter in her chest.

"Hey there. How was the rest of your travel?"

"Exhausting. But I got in at six a.m. this morning, so I had enough time to nap."

"Considering it's three o'clock in the afternoon, I would say that was more than a nap."

"Hah, basically."

It was nice to just listen to his voice, knowing that he was a little over an hour away. It was much better than him being fourteen hours away.

"Want to catch some dinner? At a restaurant. A new steak place opened in the city, and my CFO won't shut up about it."

Oh?

In all their time hanging out together, going to church, paintball matches, smash rooms and fast food runs, they'd never gone out to another restaurant together.

She supposed it was a bit weird, but it made her feel pretty good that Bryant respected that she wasn't ready to date yet. Sure, there were strange moments of electricity where it felt like they were irrevocably drawn towards each other, and occasionally he looked at her in a way that made her shiver and acutely aware of her body and exactly how much heat her face let off, but he never pressured her.

"Sure. I wouldn't mind that."

"Okay. It's fairly stuffy so wear something nice if you want."

"If I want?"

"Well, if you want to show up in a velour tracksuit, I'm sure I have enough money to bribe them to still let us in."

Keiko laughed. It seemed that Bryant grew funnier and funnier the more they got to know each other.

"You would really spend that much money just for me to go into a five-star restaurant in a sweat suit?"

"I would spend that much money just to eat with you in general."

She flushed at that. He had such a matter-of-fact way of saying compliments so easily, and it never failed to make her cheeks color.

"Wow, such a sap."

"You know it. Pick you up at seven?"

"Seven works for me."

"Great. I'll see you then."

She disconnected the call then held her phone to her chest, enjoying the excitement that bubbled through her. But after a few moments, she realized something that made her whole stomach jolt.

She only had four hours to pick an outfit and get ready.

KEIKO LOOKED AROUND in awe at the restaurant they entered into, her arm looped through Bryant's. The ceilings were high, and the lights were all incredibly fancy chandeliers, and the seats were all high quality leather.

Bryant had been right about the clientele being pretty fancy. She spotted a news anchor she saw on the TV when she was prepping coffee Sunday mornings, and she was pretty sure a model from a magazine in her dentist's office. It made her feel insecure, but then Bryant would look at her and the rest of the world faded into a dull roar.

It was a far cry from their last fancy restaurant meal, with the two of them slipping into casual conversation quickly. He told her all about his trip. She told him about the new setup she was trying for Vacation Bible School that year.

"You know, if someone would have told me a year ago that I would be sitting across from the smartest and most beautiful woman in the entire state, I probably wouldn't have believed them."

"Oh, well I don't know about all that," Keiko said, flushing slightly.

"Well, I do. And the more I get to know you, the more baffled I am by why you would ever want to hang out with me."

Her toes curled inside of her shoes. "You have your own positives, you know."

"Yeah, I guess I've been doing a little polishing on myself."

Keiko laughed, how could she not. "I wouldn't exactly say it was a little."

"What, are you saying that I needed a ton of spiffing up?"

"Well, I'm not saying it was a weekend job."

They had gotten so comfortable with each other that they could joke in a way she couldn't with anybody else but Dani, and they both shared a laugh at that.

"You're right, though. It's been a long road, but I'm proud of the man I've become. Of who I'm becoming. I suppose the challenge is now to make sure I stay on the right path."

Keiko smiled as she sipped at her drink. "I understand. Falling off the wagon happens from time to time. The important thing is that you get back on."

"I hear that." For some reason he seemed to tense.

The hairs on the back of her neck rose.

Bryant continued, "Speaking of paths and things like that, I have some big changes coming up."

"Oh?" she asked.

Like most humans, she hated change. But it also had a tendency to trigger issues with her OCD. Maybe it was the anxiety, maybe it was control issues, but either way she couldn't help the twist in her stomach.

"Yeah. I've gotten into land preservations recently."

"Uh-huh."

"And I want to build a conservation of sorts. Or a rescue of sorts. Basically, a large plot of land that I can grow trees on and cultivate native plants that have been threatened by invasive species. Take in old racehorses and abused animals, maybe wild animals that have been hurt by humans. I want to make a real difference in the world.

"And maybe, once everything is settled, we can look into training some of the rescues to be service animals."

"Wow," Keiko said, leaning back, utterly impressed. "That's... that's amazing, Bryant. I can't wait to see you do all of that."

"Yeah, I'm pretty excited too."

"I can imagine. I bet your family is too."

"Oh yeah, they definitely are, but that's probably because I bought up a huge plot of land just beyond their land so technically, we're going to be neighbors. Granted, neighbors who are really far apart, but neighbors nonetheless."

Keiko stared at him, more than a little slack-jawed. "What! Why didn't you lead with that?"

"Because," he said, a far too clever smile on his face. "I like messing with you sometimes."

"Yeah, you really do, don't you, you jerk."

"Jerk, such strong language!"

"You're lucky I'm a woman of the Lord. Otherwise your ears would be on fire right now."

"Oh, I'm sure." They were both grinning like goons, but he sobered again. "But it should put me at about twenty minutes outside of town instead of an hour thirty."

Keiko clapped her hands, not understanding why he sounded so intense. "Oh wow, you're going to be sick of me then!"

"Why do you say that?"

"Because I'm going to be over all the time. The only reason you ever got a break before is because we lived so far apart."

"What if I never wanted a break?"

"What?" she said.

His response had been so quick and subtle that she almost missed it.

"I said, what if I never wanted a break from you?" He reached across the table and took her hands in his. They were so big and warm compared to hers, covered with little burn scars from glue guns and cuts from other creative projects.

"Keiko, you're the best thing to ever happen to my life. I've learned and grown more than I could ever imagine because of you. You gave me my family back."

His eyes were locked on hers, and her blood pressure shot right up from that.

"So, since I'm going to be around enough for you to be able to rely on me for support in a much timelier fashion, I would really like to date you. Officially."

Keiko stared at him, eyes wide and heart pounding. Sure, they had been growing closer and closer with each day, but he had been playing it so cool that she had thought he only saw her as a fellow child of God and not as any sort of romantic interest. Only recently had she allowed herself to accept that *she* had romantic feelings towards him.

Her whole future played out in her mind for a minute, all the trials and tribulations. All the victories. All the failures. All those beautiful bright points that they could share together, making memories to last for generations.

She was flooded with so much, her brain feeling like it was lit up from its core and her heart doing its own special rhythm in her chest.

"Yes," she managed to whisper breathlessly. "I would like that very much."

He squeezed her hands lovingly, his smile going even broader than she thought possible. "Well then, that's the biggest stamp of approval I could ask for."

"You say that now," Keiko said, feeling like if she let go of him, she would just float off into the sky and never come down. "But wait until I show up at midnight with a Bible because I'm stuck on trying to figure out the perfect conclusion to my study."

His eyes glinted at her. "You're always welcome at my place, but perhaps it would be somewhat cruel to have me pass such a difficult test when I'm trying to be good."

Her stomach tightened. "Test? Oh!"

By the way he was looking at her, she was able to infer he meant showing up at his place of residence that late into the night. Although he and Keiko spent plenty of time together, he'd never stayed in her apartment too long after sundown.

"I'll keep that in mind," she said, keeping her eyes down. "I wouldn't want to be a bad influence on you."

At that he really did tilt his head back and laughed. "The

day that I manage to corrupt the indomitable Keiko Albryte is the day that all hope is lost for my soul."

"Indomitable, what a strange thing to call your girlfriend."

She didn't miss the jump in his expression as the words left her lips.

"Say that again," he said and leaned toward her.

"What, that indomitable is a terrible adjective for your girlfriend?"

He flashed a grin at her, and it was easy to see how he had charmed so many women before her. But that was in the past and it didn't matter. What mattered was that he was in the moment with her, the best version of himself yet.

"Yeah. You know, a guy could get used to hearing that."

"Well, behave yourself, and I just might let you."

EPILOGUE

Keiko

"All right, who's down for a ring-toss!"

Keiko sipped at her bottle of water while she glanced at Dani. "I'm so happy I put Chastity in charge of my engagement party. How did she come up with all these fun ideas? And where does she find the energy?"

Dani laughed. "I think Chastity takes this pretty hardcore."

"Did you do all this at yours?" Keiko asked.

"She was in another country when I had mine. That might or might not have been planned." Dani winked.

Keiko decided to sit out the ring-toss and take a break from all the activity. Sharing a moment with her future sisters-in-law was just as fun. Besides, Keiko was happy to be able to watch her friends and future husband enjoying themselves.

"What about you, Missy?" she asked, turning her head to

the blond who was draped over the patio love seat at the Miller Ranch.

"Back when I got engaged, Chastity was my only friend, so I wouldn't have had anyone to invite. So we didn't bother." She rubbed her hands over her large belly, her stomach even bigger than Chastity's had been when she was pregnant. "But it worked out all right, didn't it, Junior?"

"I thought you said you didn't know if it was a boy or a girl?" Dani said, her hand on her own stomach.

That action made Keiko raise her eyebrow, but she tucked that factoid in the back of her mind for another day.

"We don't, but I started calling the little bean junior, and now it stuck. If she's a girl, I'll probably just call her June or something. Anyways, Ma would like that because we can say we're naming her after Juniper, one of the Miller ancestors from so long ago."

"Ma is going to be absolutely beside herself. Little Benny is just starting to walk on his own, and there's gonna be a new baby in the house."

Keiko wrinkled her nose. "I love all of you so much, but I can't imagine all the crying."

Missy snorted, trying to sit up to grab her water but unable to get the momentum up with her belly weighing her down. After a few tries, Dani took pity on her and handed her the glass.

"Thanks. But anyway, your house with Bryant is about a ten-minute drive away from where I'll be, so it's not like it'll bother you."

"It's not my house yet," she countered, face flushing. Keiko found it difficult to think about how it would be after the wedding in a year and not also have her mind wander to what *other* things would change between her and Bryant.

It was no secret that she was inexperienced and that she had a few hang-ups with her body. But when she thought of sharing her marriage bed with the handsome and kind Miller son, she felt more excitement than fear.

...which was also pretty embarrassing, but she would have time to get over all the blushing.

A car arrived and parked in the guest area. Then the driver got out and waved. "Hello! Sorry I'm late!"

Keiko stood to see a familiar redhead arriving.

"Rosa! It's so good to see you!"

The redhead rushed forward, enveloping Keiko in a hug. "My class ran over, and my professor was just *not* the kind you ditch out early on."

"Man, is this the same professor who was giving you problems before when your babysitter fell through?"

She nodded. Wonderful Rosie had actually reached out to her a month or so after the club incident. Keiko hadn't expected that, but she'd asked if they could meet and talk more about what she had said. One thing led to another, and the next thing she knew, she and Rosa—her real name—were friends.

After that, Rosa had gone on to a GED program and then enrolled in college. She and Keiko still didn't see eye to eye on everything, but it was so wonderful to watch Rosa grow, become more confident, and demand respect for herself. She'd even started to come to Bible study right alongside Bryant, and every time Keiko saw them there, she was so proud that she thought she might burst.

"Uh-huh," Missy said from her spot on the loveseat. "Does anyone have a towel?"

"Oh, did you spill?" Keiko asked, hurrying towards the kitchen.

"Not a paper towel, a towel-towel," Missy called, her voice

rising. "And I didn't spill my water so much as I think it just broke."

Keiko had never whipped around so fast in her entire life. "Wait, *what!*"

KEIKO PACED BACK and forth just outside Missy's hospital room, her heart in her throat, her stomach somewhere in China, and her head who knew where. She was beside herself, and it was only Bryant's presence in the same hall that kept her level.

"I haven't seen you this anxious in a while," he said calmly, his voice warm and soothing. Like honey over her frayed nerves.

"Yeah, well that's because normally things aren't this dangerous or important. Do you know that America has the worst birth mortality rate of any first world country? Or all the complications that can happen? Breech birth, umbilical cord around the neck, tears, hemorrhaging!"

"Hey, hey, come over here and pray with me."

She looked back to him and he had his arms open wide for her. She went to him, resting against his chest as he enveloped her.

Gosh, his hugs had to have been sent by God because it made her feel so much safer.

"Come on, close your eyes and let's talk to God."

She did just that, his heartbeat the perfect background tempo to her prayers. Her mind raced through them at first, slowly leveling out as she calmed.

Until, of course, there was a sharp slapping sound and then a squealing cry that filled the air.

"Did she?" Keiko asked, her eyes going wide.

"I think she did," Bryant answered with a smile.

A moment later a nurse opened the door and peeked out. "The mother says that you can come in now."

That was basically enough to trigger a stampede, and the entire family that had been stuck out in the hall raced in. And there they were, little June or Junior and a very exhausted looking Missy, covered in a sheet.

Of course, later on, there was a round of pass the baby around as everyone cried and took pictures and things like that. Keiko stood back, uninterested in holding the child but just beside herself with happiness to be included in the moment.

"I'm so glad we're here for this," she murmured, wrapping her arms around Bryant.

He returned her embrace, resting his chin on her head.

"I am too. And we wouldn't be, if it weren't for you. You gave me all of this, Keiko."

She tore her eyes away from the baby long enough to stand up on her tiptoes and press a gentle kiss to his lips. Like usual, it never failed to make her head spin, and she smiled dopily.

"You gave me too much to even say," she replied.

"Well, I don't think so, but I know better than to argue with you."

"Smart man."

He pressed his own kiss to her forehead, eyes so full of love that it made her wonder if it was all a dream. "But I do know that I have so much more to give you. A whole lifetime's worth."

"I'll hold you to that."

"I hope you do."

It was in that moment, with the new life in the room and all the joy radiating from every person, that Keiko realized the full breadth of her future. The entire Miller family was together again, bringing in the next generation and spreading more love and positive change wherever they could. She'd found her purpose, that was for sure, and she couldn't wait for what else the future would bring them.

Together.

HELLO READER! I hope you enjoyed the final installment of my Brothers of Miller Ranch series!

Guess what?! I decided to write a spin-off series from this one that's all about their billionaire cousins in Texas. There's a whole lot of learning about the fact that money isn't everything in this new series, Miller Brothers of Texas! Here's book one of that new series... Humbling Her Cowboy, Miller Brothers of Texas Book One...

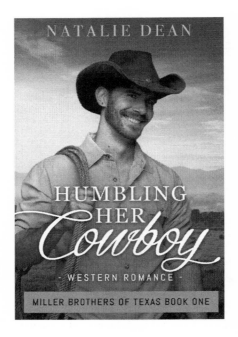

IN ADDITION, I'm super excited to tell you I'm giving the prologue of that series away for FREE! Continue on to the next page to see how to get it!

EXCLUSIVE BOOKS BY NATALIE DEAN

GET THREE FREE BOOKS when you join my Sweet Romance Newsletter :)

Get One Free Contemporary Western Romance:
The New Cowboy at Miller Ranch, Miller Brothers of Texas Prologue - He's a rich Texas rancher. She's just a tomboy ranch employee. Can she make him see life can still be happy without all that money?

AND Two Free Historical Western Romances:
Spring Rose - A feel good historical western mail-order groom novelette about a broken widow finding love and faith.

Fools Rush In- A historical western mail-order bride novelette based off a true story!

Go to nataliedeanauthor.com to find out how to join!

IF YOU ENJOYED THIS STORY...

Please be so kind as to leave an honest review. Reviews can make or break the success of a book and help readers such as yourself decide whether or not they might want to read the book. Even if you only write a few words, it makes a big difference! Thank you so much...

OTHER BOOKS BY NATALIE DEAN

NATALIE DEAN

MILLER BROTHERS OF TEXAS (Contemporary)

Humbling Her Cowboy

In Debt to the Cowboy

The Cowboy Falls for the Veterinarian

More Coming Soon!

BROTHERS OF MILLER RANCH (Contemporary)

Her Second Chance Cowboy

Saving Her Cowboy

Her Rival Cowboy

Her Fake-Fiance Cowboy Protector

Taming Her Cowboy Billionaire

BROTHERS OF MILLER RANCH BOX SET

MARRYING A MARSHAL SERIES (Historical)

An Unexpected Treasure

The Dangers of Love

The Outlaw's Daughter

Falling for the Marshal

No Time For Love

MARRYING A MARSHAL BOX SET (includes the above five books, plus the previously unreleased 6th book of my Marrying a Marshal series)

LAWMEN'S BRIDES SERIES (Historical)

The Ranger's Wife

Benjamin's Bride

Carson's Christmas Bride

Justin's Captive Bride

BRIDES AND TWINS SERIES (Historical)

A Soldier's Love

Taming the Rancher

The Wrong Bride

A Surprise Love

The Last Sister's Love

BRIDES & TWINS Box Set / Mail-Order Bride Compilation (My bestseller! It includes TWO MORE unreleased heartwarming mail-order bride series)

LOVE ON THE TRAILS SERIES (Historical)

A Love Beyond Suspicion

Picture Perfect Love

Love of a Wild Rose

A Dangerous Time to Love

A Cold Winter's Love

Brides, Trails, and Mountain Men

Historical Western Romance Compilation

Includes my *Love on the Trails Series* plus an exclusive series titled *Marrying a Mountain Man*

BOULDER BRIDES SERIES (Historical)

The Teacher's Bride

The Independent Bride

The Perfect Bride

The Indian's Bride

The Civil War Bride

BOULDER BRIDES BOX SET

BRIDES OF BANNACK SERIES (Historical)

Lottie

Cecilia

Sarah

Though I try to keep this list updated in each book, you may also visit my website nataliedeanauthor.com for the most up to date information on my book list.

ABOUT AUTHOR - NATALIE DEAN

Born and raised in a small coastal town in the south I realized at a young age that I was more adventurous than my conservative friends and family. I loved to travel. My passion for travel opened up a whole new world and new cultures to me that I will always be grateful for.

I was raised to treasure family. I always knew that at some point in my life I would leave my storybook life behind and become someone's mother, someone's aunt and hopefully someone's grandmother. Little did I know that the birth of my son later in life would make me the happiest I've ever been. He will always be my biggest achievement. The strong desire to be a work-from-home mom is what lead me down this path of publishing books.

While I have always loved reading I never realized how much I would love writing until I started. I feel like each one of my books have been influenced by someone or something I've experienced in my life. To be able to share this gift has become a dream come true.

I hope you enjoy reading them as much as I have enjoyed creating them. I truly hope to develop an ongoing relationship with all of my readers that lasts into my last days :)

www.nataliedeanauthor.com

Made in the USA
Coppell, TX
08 November 2020